BACK TO PASS

by
Lisa M. Bolt Simons

Minneapolis, Minnesota

DEDICATION

To former football player, football coach, and my husband, Dave.

ACKNOWLEDGEMENTS

Thanks to Ned L., Isaac S., and Lexi T. for sharing your football expertise. Thanks, as well, to Nick K. for the constant reminder about the other book. This one is for you.

Edited by Ryan Jacobson
Game design and "How to Use This Book" by Ryan Jacobson
Cover art by Elizabeth Hurley

Author photograph by Jillian Raye Photography. The following images used under license from Shutterstock.com: enterlinedesign (football field), Michal Sanca (football player), Route55 (football), sirtravelalot (promotional photograph), and tele52 (helmet)

Copyright 2017 by Lisa M. Bolt Simons
Published by Lake 7 Creative, LLC
Minneapolis, MN 55412
www.lake7creative.com

ISBN: 978-1-940647-27-2; eISBN: 978-1-940647-28-9

TABLE OF CONTENTS

HOW TO USE THIS BOOK

As you read *Back to Pass*, your goal is simple: make it to the happy ending on page 154. It's not as easy as it sounds. You will sometimes be asked to jump to a distant page. Please follow these instructions. Sometimes you will be asked to choose between two or more options. Decide which you feel is best, and go to the corresponding page. (Be careful; some options will lead to disaster.) Finally, if a page offers no instructions or choices, simply continue to the next page.

EARN POINTS

Along the way, you will sometimes collect points for your decisions. Points are awarded for

A) confidence,
B) skill,
C) speed, and
D) teamwork.

Keep track of your points using a bookmark that you can cut out on page 157 (or on a separate piece of paper). You'll need the points later on.

TALENT SCORE

Before you begin, you must determine your talent score. This number stands for the natural ability that your character, Jesse, was born with. The number will not change during the story. You can get your talent score in one of three ways:

Quick Way: Give yourself a talent score of two.

Standard Way: If you have any dice, roll one die. The number that you roll is your talent score. (You only get one try. So if you roll a one, you're stuck with it.)

Fun Way: Get a parent or guardian's help (to make sure you're in a safe place where no one—and nothing—can be hurt or damaged). Find a partner to play catch with you. Stand 20 steps apart. Gently toss a rubber ball back and forth six times. This gives you six tries to catch the ball. Every time you catch it, you get a point. You only get six tries, whether the throws are on target or not. If you miss all six, that's okay. As long as you're a good sport and don't get mad, give yourself one talent point for trying the *Fun Way*. Give yourself one skill point, too. After all, skill gets better with practice.

STARTING OFFENSE

MICHAEL JANDRO
wide receiver

TRUC NGUYEN
tackle

CONNOR JUSTIN
running back

SANTIAGO RAMIREZ
guard

BRADY SANCHEZ
quarterback

NICK HELTON
center

MASON POMMER
guard

MITCHELL COMBS
running back

RAMSEY HURLEY
tackle

WALKER DECLANE
tight end

KYLE SHAFFER
wide receiver

-10 -20 -30 -40

STARTING DEFENSE

J.T. LOCKWOOD
cornerback

KYLE SHAFFER
safety

WEN NATHAN
defensive end

WALKER DECLANE
outside linebacker

TRUC NGUYEN
defensive tackle

MITCHELL COMBS
middle linebacker

RAMSEY HURLEY
defensive tackle

STAN COLMILLO
outside linebacker

JEFF RILEY
defensive end

BRIAN CHRISTIE
safety

CONNOR JUSTIN
cornerback

PROLOGUE

Author's note: Do you have your talent points yet? If not, please read pages 4–5.

It's fourth down and goal to go. The ball is just three yards from the end zone—three yards from the win. Your team is trailing, 20–24. You need a touchdown; you need those six points for victory. You glance at the scoreboard. The clock ticks under its final minute. This is your team's last chance. As the quarterback, it's up to you to win it. Championships are never easy.

Coach wants you to fake a handoff to the running back, keep the football, and run it into the end zone. You've done this before. It might work. It *will* work.

You call the play in the huddle, and then your team lines up. You walk to the line of scrimmage, and you scan the defense. You see an opening. You know what to do. You know where to run.

You glance at your parents in the bleachers. Your mom smiles widely. Sitting next to her, your dad nods. "You can do it!" he yells.

More yells come from both sides. It mostly sounds like garbled noise, but every once in a while, you hear a distinct cheer.

"Go, Gators!"

"Run the ball!"

The only voices that matter right now are yours and your coach's.

Go to the next page.

You put your hands under the center. As you do, the defense shifts. The players change positions. They crowd the line of scrimmage. The hole that you were going to run through closes up. The other team knows you're going to run the football. They're expecting it.

A quarterback knows how to call an audible—how to change the play at the last second. But this is the championship. Your coach knows more about the game than you do. Should you trust his call and do what he says? The running play still might work. Or should you audible to a pass and do what the defense doesn't expect? What will you choose to do?

To run the football, go to page 60.

To pass the football, go to page 27.

You're embarrassed, but you haven't done anything wrong—not really. You pull back your hand, spin away from the table, and walk as fast as you can. You weave around chairs and tables with no problems. Just as you get to the edge of the street, you hear the man's voice.

"Young man, wait a second!"

His tone of voice startles you. It doesn't sound mad. In fact, the man almost sounds . . . kind. You can't help yourself. You look over your shoulder at him.

He's walking, not running, toward you. "Don't go," he says. "My daughter changed her mind about the muffin. She wants a lemon poppy seed. I'd hate to waste this one. Would you like to have it?"

You look at him again. He holds a napkin-wrapped bundle out to you.

You quickly glance in both directions to make sure no cars are coming. Then you nod slightly, grab the muffin, and run before he can change his mind.

AWARD YOURSELF 1 TEAMWORK POINT.

Go to page 22.

If you go with your uncle, you'll finally be off the streets. You'll have food, shelter, and safety. But what if Gary isn't such a nice guy? You've never lived with him; you don't know what he's like. Besides, you haven't had to worry about anyone else for a year. Do you even want to move in with someone?

"Uncle Gary, I'm not sure," you say. "I need to think about it."

"No worries," he says. "I just want to make sure you're safe."

"I'm fine. I've been on my own for a year. I know how to take care of myself."

Uncle Gary nods. "Okay, do you have a phone?"

You pull the broken one out of your backpack. "I got it out of the trash. It doesn't work. But I bet they'd let me use the library phone." You take out a notebook and a pen and hand them to your uncle. "If you write down your number, I'll call you later."

"I have a cell phone," he says. "I'm not good at checking it all the time, but I get voice messages. I'll give you my work number, too. That's actually why I came to the library. They were having problems with their basement lights, so I was fixing them." He finishes writing and hands back the notebook.

"Is there any way I can get in touch with you?" he asks. "Just in case."

"Leave a message for me with a librarian. The one who knows me the best is Delane."

He smiles and pats your shoulder. "I'll try not to pressure you. I'm just thinking what would be best for you and all."

"Yeah, I know," you tell him.

You don't believe it, but you feel sort of sad when Uncle Gary leaves. You only spent a short time together, but it was nice to be with someone familiar.

For the rest of the afternoon and evening, you look for a place to sleep. All of your usual spots are taken.

You finally curl up in the doorway of a gym where the light is out. You put your backpack under your head, using it as a pillow. It helps a little, but it does nothing against the chilly night.

Your uncle could never replace your mom, but he has blankets . . . and a bed . . . and food.

You'll call him tomorrow.

Go to page 33.

You feel bad about lying to your friends and teammates, but it's better this way. You weren't in Japan, but you did go to the library almost every day and taught yourself a lot. You learned current events by reading newspapers, and you practiced math and science online. You also tried coding a website, just for fun. The only thing you're behind on is . . . writing.

You shrug. "After my mom died, I lived in Japan with some relatives."

Santiago's mouth drops open. "Really? Wow! What's it like there? Are the schools different? How's the food? Did you make any friends? Did you have a girlfriend?"

Uh, oh. This lie might backfire. Time to change the subject—fast.

"Oh, it's not really that interesting. But, hey, I'm here now," you say with a smile.

Santiago slaps your shoulder. "Glad to have you. Are you gonna join the team?"

"Hopefully, today," you reply. "My uncle needs to turn in the paperwork."

Go to the next page.

When lunch ends, Santiago stands. He's grown even bigger. Huge. "See you at practice," he says.

"Totally." You feel as if you've just run onto the field, right before the start of a game. You're pumped up and ready to go.

Go to page 52.

Another football player hit the kicker. *Hit.* An illegal play. Yet the best way to help Briley and your team is to ignore it.

You jog over to Briley and help her up. When you turn, you see a few of your teammates surrounding the guilty Canton player. No one does anything but stare the kid down. Plus, the referee blows his whistle like crazy to make sure nothing else happens.

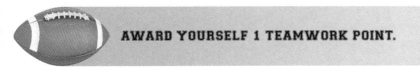

AWARD YOURSELF 1 TEAMWORK POINT.

As both teams retreat to their benches, the ref calls a "roughing the kicker" penalty on Canton. Your team gets an extra 15 yards when you kick the ball to them.

This was a strong showing of team spirit, and it should fire up the Gators even more. Instead, the play seems to wake the sleeping Coyotes.

During the third quarter, the opposing team gets the ball three times. They score a touchdown and add a two-point conversion all three times, tying the score at 24.

"What's going on here?" Coach snaps. "The first half, you guys were sailing like captains of the ship. The second half, you're mopping the deck. The game isn't over. Get it together!"

The fourth quarter doesn't start much better. On your first offensive play, the center fumbles the snap. On your next play, Connor fumbles, too.

Coach Louis yells so loudly at the team that you worry he'll snap his vocal cords.

You glance at the stands. Your uncle is sitting up too straight, as if he's wearing a back brace. Every muscle in his body looks tense. You know how he feels.

With only a minute to go, the Gators get the ball at the 40-yard line. There's time for one more drive, if the team hurries.

Brady connects on an eight-yard pass to Kyle. Then Connor gets a screen pass out of the backfield and runs for 15 yards. Kyle gets open again, and Brady fires a throw to him. This one goes for 19 yards.

"Time out," Brady yells.

The ball sits at the 18-yard line. The clock reads 0:04. There is only time for one more play. The odds are against scoring a touchdown, but a field goal is possible, especially with Briley kicking.

The coach agrees. "Field goal!" he yells.

Before Briley runs onto the field, she glances at you. You simply nod and give her a thumbs up.

The center snaps the ball. The holder places it on the ground. Briley quickly steps forward and kicks.

The football soars into the air. It drifts left . . . drifts left . . . drifts left . . .

You hold your breath. The moment seems to last all night. Finally, the ball passes through, barely nicking the goal post.

The official in the end zone nods and holds his arms in the air. The kick is good! The Gators win!

Behind you, the crowd erupts into cheers. All the players on the sideline start to join in.

"Stop!" Coach Louis demands. "There will be no celebrating tonight's performance."

Sure, a win is a win, but how your team played is not a good way to start the season. You will not win many more games unless you all improve.

Go to the next page.

When you get to English class on Monday, your teacher collects the homework assignment—except you didn't do it. You were supposed to read *Maniac Magee* and answer five questions about it. You enjoyed the book, and you could answer questions perfectly in your mind. But you couldn't write them down.

"What do you think about the book?" your teacher, Mrs. Meyer, asks you.

"It's good."

"It's still one of my favorites." She looks at the pile of homework and then at you. "Just put your assignment in the pile and have a seat."

This is embarrassing, and it could get you kicked off the football team. If your teachers—and Uncle Gary—find out that you can't write, they might make you take extra classes instead of going to practice! Should you give her an excuse and get Briley to help you? Or should you admit your problem? What will you choose to do?

To get help from Briley, go to page 76.

To admit that you can't write, go to page 38.

You're embarrassed, but you haven't done anything wrong—not really. Yet you're hungry. So hungry.

Part of you knows it's wrong to steal, but another part of you knows that you need to eat. Without much thought, you lean forward and snatch the muffin off the table. You hear the man gasp, but you don't wait around to hear anything else.

You spin away from the table and run as fast as you can—straight into the waiter standing behind you. You tumble to the ground and feel a sting in your elbow as it scrapes against the pavement.

As quickly as possible, you climb to your feet. That's when you hear the man's voice.

"Young man, wait a second!"

His tone startles you. It doesn't sound mad. In fact, the man almost sounds . . . kind. You can't help yourself. You look over your shoulder at him.

He's walking, not running, toward you. He looks at you with such sadness and pity—probably taking in your thin face and dirty clothes.

"Don't go," he says. "My daughter was just telling me she changed her mind about the muffin. She wants a lemon poppy seed. We were going to take the blueberry one home, but you're welcome to have it."

You study him closely, wondering if this is some sort of trick. His soft eyes and gentle smile suggest that he is sincere.

You quickly glance in both directions to make sure no cars are coming. Then you nod slightly and run away before he can change his mind.

Go to the next page.

You go to the library and sit on the short brick wall that borders the parking lot. There, you savor every bite of the blueberry muffin. Then, with your belly as full as it's been in days, you venture inside.

You like coming here. It's one of your favorite spots in town. The library offers an escape from days that are too hot, too cold, or too rainy. Plus, you love to read. Graphic novels are your favorite, but you also enjoy science fiction and sports biographies.

You have your nose in *Out of My Mind* when you hear someone say your name. You look up, expecting to see a librarian. But it's not a librarian. It's your dad's brother, your Uncle Gary.

"I thought that was you," he says. His voice is quiet. His hair looks gray, and he's thinner than the last time you saw him. He wears a tool belt. "I've been looking all over for you. Ever since you . . . ran away."

You don't say anything. You're too afraid. Will he turn you in to social services? Or will he be cool? Maybe he'll walk away and leave you alone.

He doesn't say anything else. He only stands there with his hands in his pockets. He's been looking for you. But now that he found you, he seems nervous.

"I should apologize for my brother," your uncle says. "He shouldn't have left you and your mom."

You nod.

He smiles widely, as if an idea just came to him. "Say, I bet you're hungry. I know I am. How about I take you out for pizza? That was always your favorite, right? It will give us a chance to talk."

Your mouth waters at the mention of *pizza*. You can't remember the last time you ate a full meal. But can you trust him? Is this really just a free lunch? Or is it a trick? Maybe he's planning to take you to social services—or even all the way to Minnesota. What will you choose to do?

To eat lunch with your uncle, go to page 56.

To say, "No, thanks," go to page 71.

You'd like to accept your uncle's offer, but waiting will only make it harder to go back. You think of your favorite football coach. He always said never to avoid challenges. He was right.

"Uncle Gary, you don't have to call. I'll go today."

He drops you off, and you head into school. Your heart pounds like you just ran a mile.

So many people ask where you've been. It's like you weren't even there yesterday. Maybe they were too nervous to ask. Maybe they didn't think you'd come back. Or maybe they didn't recognize you. Whatever the reason, they waited for today, and it's a downpour of questions.

By lunchtime, you've had enough. Uncle Gary said you didn't have to come, so he won't mind if you leave. You sneak out of school and walk a mile or so to the community center.

You play basketball for a while, but you aren't very good at it. You keep missing shots. Maybe lifting weights will help you to feel better.

You go to the bench press. You're so upset that you put more weights on the bar than you probably should. Then you lie on your back and slide underneath it. You manage to push the bar up once and down again. On the way up a second time, you feel a sharp stab of pain in your left shoulder. Without thinking, you jerk your arm down, and the bar slips off balance. It tips to the side, and your right arm buckles. The weight is too much to hold. The bar slams down hard against your chest. *Crack!* The pain is like nothing you've ever felt before.

You can't get the bar off your body. You cry out in fear and helplessness. Fortunately, it isn't long before someone comes in, gets the bar off you, and calls 911.

You don't remember much else until you wake up. You feel light-headed, numb, like that time you had a tooth pulled at the dentist's office. The only sensation you notice is in your chest. It feels heavy, like the entire Atlanta Falcons football team is sitting on it.

"Hey, there," says Uncle Gary. He looks worried.

You try to ask, "What happened?" but it sounds more like a groan.

"Take it easy, Jesse," he says, holding out his hand as if to say, *stop*. "You have two broken ribs. A few others are cracked. So try not to move, okay?"

It takes a moment for the news to set in. When it does, you close your eyes to hold back the tears. No more football.

Go to page 79.

The center made a mistake. It's too risky to pitch the football with so many defenders so close. The right play is to keep it and try to score.

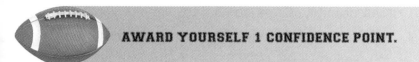

AWARD YOURSELF 1 CONFIDENCE POINT.

Three defensive players surround you, but you spin and run backward. As you zip past Connor, he launches himself at the defenders—and blocks two of them.

You cut and scoot by the third defender, but you trip. You stumble . . . regain your balance, and sprint into the end zone. The Gators lead, 26–21!

The fans roar in celebration, but there are still two minutes to play. That's a long time in a football game.

The defense plays tough, though. They sack the quarterback and force a fumble. A mix of defensive and offensive linemen pile on top of it. When the referees sort out the players, Truc is holding the football.

The Gators win again!

Go to page 101.

Your coach called the play, but he didn't expect them to be in this kind of defense. He would want you to change the play—so that's what you'll do.

"Twin 92," you shout. *Twin* is your team's secret word for audible, and *92* is the number for a pass play to your favorite wide receiver, Brady Sanchez.

"28! 9! 28!" you yell.

Nick Helton snaps the ball to you, and everyone on your team springs into action. You scoot back and hold the ball out for Connor Justin, the team's best running back. He pretends to take it from you.

You spin around and look for Brady. He's open, but a big defensive tackle breaks through your offensive line. You have to run away from him.

As you sprint toward the sideline, you spin the ball to Brady. The pass is on target. Brady sticks out his hands to catch it—just as a cornerback dives in front of him and swats the ball to the ground.

A referee blows his whistle, and the play is over.

It doesn't matter how close you were. You've lost the championship game.

1

RUNAWAY

Your name is Jesse Allan. You've played football for most of your life. There's even a picture of you as a baby, lying with a football next to you. You also remember a picture of your cub football team when you were eight years old. You don't know where those pictures are, not anymore, not when you're living in whichever car, back porch, or shelter you can find.

Dad left you and Mom about a week after your football season ended. He wrote a note saying that he was sorry and that he didn't want to let you and Mom down anymore. You didn't know what he meant by that. You still don't.

That was six months before Mom got sick. You're not even sure if Dad knows she got cancer.

When she died, he wasn't there. Some of Mom's relatives came all the way from Japan, but Dad never showed up.

With him gone, Mom had arranged for you to live with her cousin in Minnesota. But you didn't want to leave Georgia, so you ran away from home.

That was over a year ago.

You can't go to school now, or they'd force you to move away. Instead, you spend your days searching for a free meal. Some days, you're lucky enough to find something good, like leftover pizza. On the bad days, you don't eat at all.

When you're not worrying about meals, you have to figure out where to sleep. It's a challenge to find places that are safe and warm. *Safe* is more important than *warm*, though. There are tricks for warming up chilly places. Old newspapers aren't great blankets, but they are better than nothing.

Go to the next page.

You slept on a park bench last night. Dinner was the final three bites of someone's mostly eaten hamburger. You found it on top of a trash bag behind Jack's Family Restaurant. That's better than what you had for breakfast this morning: nothing.

You gaze across the street. The clock inside the local coffee shop says it's 11:15 a.m. You sit down on the curb, straight across from the dining tables outside the shop. You pull the cell phone out of your backpack. It doesn't work, but it's good for pretending to text family and friends—if only you had any. The phone makes you seem like you belong there, while you wait . . . and watch.

It's a nice day. Autumn is coming, cooling things off a bit. Plenty of customers are sitting at the tables. Most are only drinking coffee, but some are eating. Those are the people you're interested in.

Your stomach grumbles. You think of all the times you used to say, "I'm starving" before lunch at school.

You had no idea.

A man with three young kids catches your attention. They're enjoying the shop's famous blueberry muffins. A lone parent out with more than one child is an easy target for someone as sneaky as you.

You stroll across the street. As you get close to their table, one of the kids drops her napkin on the ground.

Her dad leans over to pick it up. Now is your chance. You reach out to grab the biggest muffin left. But the dad is quicker than you thought he'd be. He swings back up and sets the napkin on the table. The smile drops off his face as he locks eyes with you. He stares, and you stare back. You're almost as surprised as he seems to be.

Should you forget about the muffin and walk away? You haven't done anything wrong yet. Or should you grab it and run? You're so hungry, and there's no way he is faster than you are. What will you choose to do?

To leave now, go to page 11.

To take the muffin, go to page 20.

You think about the past year of your life. You've had a hard time finding places to sleep. It's been even harder finding things to eat. You're tired of living without a home, without a family. You know what choice to make, and you know your mom would approve.

"Okay, I guess we should give it a try," you say.

Uncle Gary's eyes brighten. "That's great, Jesse. I'm happy to hear it. It'll be a fresh start for both of us." His smile fades. He scratches his head like he's not sure what to do. "Well, uh, I suppose we should get your stuff."

You can't help but grin. "Uncle Gary, this backpack is all I have."

His cheeks turn rosy. "Oh, yeah, I suppose so."

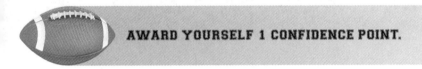

AWARD YOURSELF 1 CONFIDENCE POINT.

"I have to get back to work, soon. That's why I came to the library. I was fixing some lights in the basement. But I can drop you off at my place first."

"Okay," you say. You hope this isn't a bad idea.

2

A FRESH START

Uncle Gary lives in a small house near the edge of town, and it's clean. It actually reminds you a bit of your old house with its built-in bookcases and aqua kitchen counter tops.

Uncle Gary shows you to a room with a desk and a twin-sized bed. He tells you that your dad stayed here for a few weeks after he left your mom.

You don't want to hear about that.

"Tomorrow, I'll take you to school. We can sign you up for football, if you want. You've probably only missed a couple weeks of practice."

Football sounds exciting. School sounds terrifying. You have lots of bad memories. You can read just fine;

you enjoy it, in fact. But you can't write. The ideas in your head won't come out through your pencil.

You remember so many times, sitting frustrated in front of a blank page. Your grades were never the best, and you told Mom writing wasn't your favorite subject.

At conferences, when your teachers mentioned it, your parents frowned at you. Then they took in the good news: "Your son is polite and works hard. He's also very kind to his classmates." All was forgiven.

Uncle Gary makes spaghetti for dinner, and it's the best you've ever tasted. You don't eat much, though. You made that mistake at a community dinner after you hadn't eaten for a few days. You got a stomachache that lasted all night.

When you climb into bed, you remember how good it feels to be in an actual bed, a real pillow under your head. You relax, close your eyes, and drift to sleep.

Go to the next page.

In the morning, Gary makes pancakes and gives you a new backpack with some school supplies inside. Then he drives you to school. Just walking in the doors makes you want to throw up—you're that anxious.

Uncle Gary registers you, promises to sign you up for football, and you walk to your first class.

The entire day, your stomach feels like it's been hit by a linebacker, but you manage to get through it.

As school ends, you're called to the office. Gary is waiting for you there.

"Sorry, Jesse, you can't go to football practice, yet," he says. "There's a lot of paperwork to fill out, but we'll get it done."

He drops you off at his house—*your* house. "Grab a snack if you want," he says. "I'll get us some chicken and be home about 5:30 or 6."

It's weird to think that you have a home—and that someone is bringing you food.

After a delicious dinner, you plop down on the couch with your book.

"Any homework?" Gary asks.

"Not yet," you lie. In truth, your English teacher said something about everyone writing a short story. Not good.

You go to bed earlier than you need to, but you can't wait to get in between those sheets and have a pillow under your head. Sleep comes quickly. You dream about throwing up before playing in a football game.

Go to the next page.

When you awaken, that barfy feeling remains. It's not because of football, though. You don't want to go back to school—back to English class.

At breakfast, you pick at your scrambled eggs.

"What's up?" Gary asks.

"Uh . . . I'm not real excited about school."

"Yeah, I suppose. It's probably tough after being gone for so long."

You nod, but you don't want to explain how hard writing is, how dumb it makes you feel.

"I'll tell you what," Gary says. "If you don't want to go today, I get it. It might take some time to adjust. Things are probably really weird right now. I'll just call and let them know. Does that sound good?"

You appreciate Gary's offer. But if you don't start going, it won't ever get better. Then again, you feel overwhelmed. A day off might help you to focus—and keep you out of trouble. What will you choose to do?

To attend school, go to page 24.

To stay home, go to page 68.

It would be best to tell your teacher. Maybe she can help you, right? Besides, football is important to you, but so is getting an education.

"Mrs. Meyer . . ."

How do you start? What should you say? Well, you might as well get to the point.

"I can't write," you blurt.

"What do you mean?" She can't be any older than your mom would be. When she frowns, a few small wrinkles show beside her eyes.

"I can't write. I mean, I guess I can, sort of. But it takes me a long time, and it's really hard. What I think in my mind I can't put on paper. And my handwriting is hard to read, and my spelling . . . I can't spell."

Mrs. Meyer thinks for a moment. Then she asks, "Does reading bother you?"

"No, I love reading. But it's kind of weird. I have a hard time reading maps and seeing the shapes, I guess."

She pats your arm. "Thank you for telling me, Jesse. First, I want you to know this isn't weird. Issues like these are more common than you might think. If you don't mind, I'll talk to some of the other teachers and see what's best to do about this."

"Okay," you say.

Your hands are shaking. Your chest feels tight. Yes, telling her was one of the scariest things you've done in a long time. But you're glad that you did. You leave the classroom feeling lighter, like a bunch of pressure has been taken off your shoulders.

You're surprised that you actually feel hopeful—and even a little excited. Maybe there's a chance you can learn to write. That would be amazing.

5

NEW ASSIGNMENT

Before your mom got cancer, she taught you the three Japanese alphabets: *Kanji*, *Hiragana*, and *Katakana*. Although she tried to teach you how to write "Jesse" in *Katakana*, you couldn't figure out the lines and shapes.

You sincerely hope that Mrs. Meyer will be able to help. You can't avoid writing for the rest of your life.

Uncle Gary makes you waffles for breakfast. "My favorite thing," he says, "is putting whipped cream on top. But at family reunions, get the can before your cousin Mark. He's a whipped cream hog."

You smile at the thought of so much whipped cream on a waffle. "Sure, I'll try it," you say.

"Now, that's the Allan family spirit."

He squirts the whipped cream in a couple of circles on top of your waffle. Then he lines his finger with it. "Your dad used to put the can in his mouth," he says before licking his finger.

You laugh out loud. "I remember. My mom always got mad at him for that."

Gary sits at the table and tells you more stories about your dad. Some of them surprise you, but you find that you like hearing about him.

At school, Mrs. Meyer tells your class about the next *Maniac Magee* assignment. You accidentally groan out loud, causing a few of the kids around you to snicker.

"Hang on," Mrs. Meyer says, looking right at you. "Let me get through all of the explanation. Then we'll see if it's still groan-able."

The class laughs.

"The assignment is to compare *Maniac Magee* with a famous person. This person can be anyone in history, living or dead. The original assignment calls for writing an essay—"

You groan very quietly this time.

"—or you can pick another way to complete it: a video of yourself, a speech in class, photographs, or artwork. Feel free to get creative. Grading will be the same for everyone, no matter which way you choose. The handout I'll be giving you should better explain your options."

Your body relaxes, and you breathe easier. You are thankful that your teacher gave the class other options. But you still have to solve your writing problem, sooner or later.

"Before we start practice," Coach Louis says, "I want to walk through some problems I saw in the game."

The players split into an offense and a defense. Coach leads everyone through a handful of plays, time and again. He points out what is supposed to happen versus what did happen.

"Let's get to some drills," Coach decides. "Offense, I want the Gauntlet Drill. Defense, grab the sled and work on that." He looks at you. "Jesse, let's have a chat."

Go to the next page.

You pull off your helmet. "Yeah, Coach?"

"I've been thinking: You show potential at receiver, but you have more experience as a quarterback. So, I'm wondering if you want to stay at wide receiver. Or would you rather move to backup quarterback?"

"You're giving me a choice?" you ask.

"Yes, I think that's fair. I know quarterback is your position of choice. But chances are you'll play more at wide receiver. Either way, I need to know. What will you choose to do?"

To stay at wide receiver, go to page 80.

To be the backup quarterback, go to page 63.

Briley was never quiet or shy, but that didn't mean she couldn't keep a secret. You do remember that Briley was a good friend. But you don't want to talk about the past year, not yet.

"I'm sorry, Briley, but I'd rather you didn't ask. It's something I'll keep to myself for now."

"Okay," she agrees.

"Don't take it personally," you add. "When I'm ready to talk, you'll be the first person to know."

"Sounds good."

"Anyway, I'm ready to play football, now," you say, switching subjects. "I'm excited to be on your team. But you know this is American football, right? It's not *fútbol*, you soccer queen."

She playfully punches your arm, and you walk off the big, green field together.

4
GAME NIGHT

Fridays are supposed to be good days. But it's been a horrible one at school—almost as if all the teachers got together and planned an entire day focused on your greatest weakness: writing. In science, you had to take lab notes. Social studies required you to write a new Declaration of Independence for the year 2100. Even in math—a class that is supposed to be about numbers— you were told to write your own word problems.

At least it's over. Now, you should be nervous for your first football game, but you're too busy feeling ticked off about school. You're not dumb. You read—a lot. You work on the computer. But being asked to write makes you feel like you're in a different country where you don't know the language.

Your mom knew two languages—totally smart. Dad was, too. He worked as an electrician, like Uncle Gary. He also took business classes in college. What happened to you? Why is writing so hard?

You're standing by the locker room door when Briley turns the corner.

"You'll get dressed faster if you actually go into the locker room," she jokes.

You try to force a smile; your mood won't allow it.

"What's wrong?" she asks.

"Bad day."

"Sorry, Jesse." After a pause, Briley adds, "The good news is we're playing the Canton Coyotes. They kind of stink. It should be an easy win for us."

You shrug. "I hope so."

"I'll see you out on the field." She takes a few steps away and then turns around. "Glad you're back, Jesse."

Go to the next page.

When you get to the field, you look for Uncle Gary in the stands. He said that he was going to sit in the middle section, up near the top row. That's exactly where he is. Tina sits next to him. You give them a quick wave. You're sad that your parents aren't here, but at least someone came to watch you.

After the national anthem, the Gators offense runs onto the field. Michael Jandro and Kyle Shaffer are the starting wide receivers, so you study them closely.

You're glad to be back on the team, but it feels weird to sit on the sidelines while the offense is on the field. Brady sails a deep pass to Michael for a touchdown, and those weird feelings disappear as you celebrate with your teammates. Briley kicks the extra point, and the Gators lead, 7–0.

The defense takes its turn, ripping into the Coyotes' backfield with a quarterback sack. Two plays later, the Canton quarterback throws a pass that's tipped at the line of scrimmage. It falls into the hands of your middle linebacker, Mitchell Combs, for an interception!

The offense starts at the Coyotes' 38-yard line. Brady hands off to Connor Justin, who slams through a tackler and gains seven yards.

Brady hands the football to him again, and again. Canton cannot stop him. On his fourth carry, he breaks free from two Canton players and zooms into the end zone for a touchdown. Briley adds another point, and the score is 14–0.

The Coyotes can't catch a break. On their second play, Ramsey Hurley sacks the quarterback, who fumbles the football. Truc Nguyen seems to be the only player to spot the loose ball. He sprints toward it and swan dives onto it. Just like that, the Gators take over on offense.

Brady leads the offense down the field with a steady mix of running and passing plays. With 34 seconds left in the first quarter, Brady zips a 20-yard pass to Michael in the middle of the end zone. Touchdown!

What a way to close out a quarter. The Gator sideline buzzes with energy.

Go to the next page.

Coach Louis puts you in for the second quarter. When the Gators get back on offense, the first two plays are runs. But on third down, Brady calls a pass play in the huddle.

When the ball is snapped, you fake a slant pattern into the middle of the field and spin toward the sideline. It's such a good move that the cornerback falls down, leaving you wide open.

Brady fires a perfect pass into your stomach. You feel it slip between your arms; you see it bounce on the ground in front of you. You dropped it. That means it's fourth down; your team has to punt the ball away.

Coach doesn't say anything when you get back to the bench. He doesn't have to. You feel terrible that you messed up such an easy play.

Lucky for you, the defense covers for your mistake. They force another Canton interception and return it all the way to the 12-yard line.

It should be a quick touchdown for the Gators, but three straight running plays net just two yards.

On fourth down, there's still a chance to add three points to your score if Briley can make a field goal. Her special teams unit rushes onto the field, and you take your place at the left end of the line. Your job is simple: block the Canton player across from you.

You do your job well. You don't see Briley's kick, but you hear it. That means the play is over. You look up at the goal posts and watch the football sail between them. The kick is good, making the score 24–0.

You spin toward Briley—only to see her tackled by the player you were blocking! It was a dirty play. He was trying to hurt her. Maybe it's because they're behind by 24 points, or maybe it's because she's a girl and he's a bully. Either way, your fists clench.

You shouldn't let him get away with that. Briley is a teammate and a friend, and it's your job to defend her. Then again, this is a game. The referees are supposed to keep cheap shots like that from happening. Maybe you should pretend like you never saw it and hope the refs deal with the matter. What will you choose to do?

To defend Briley, go to page 72.

To pretend you didn't see it, go to page 16.

You feel bad about lying to your friends and teammates, but it's better this way. Besides, it's not much of a lie. It's kind of true; you went to the library almost every day and taught yourself a lot. You homeschooled yourself—just without the *home*. You learned current events by reading newspapers, and you practiced math and science online. You also tried coding a website for fun. The only thing you're behind on is . . . writing.

You shrug. "After my mom died, I was homeschooled for a while. But, hey, I'm back now," you say with a smile, hoping to change the subject.

Santiago slaps your back. "Glad to have you. Are you gonna join the team?"

"Hopefully, today," you reply. "My uncle needs to turn in the paperwork."

When lunch ends, Santiago stands. He's grown even bigger. Huge. "See you at practice," he says.

"Totally." You feel as if you've just run onto the field, right before the start of a game. You're pumped up and ready to go.

AWARD YOURSELF 1 TEAMWORK POINT.

3
FIRST PRACTICE

The afternoon feels like you're sludging through corn syrup—you cannot wait to get back on the football field. You missed a year, but it feels like a dozen.

When you head to the locker room, you're so excited that you forget how nervous you've been.

"Jesse!" Santiago calls.

You give him a quick wave.

"Hey, Jesse." Coach Tyler Louis motions you over, and you follow him to his office. He's so tall that you wonder if he used to play basketball, too. "Take a seat for a minute."

Coach Louis is new to Rosso. Uncle Gary told you he was a football coach at another school for more than 15 years. He's generally done well with his teams.

He leans back in his chair. "What position do you want to play?"

"I always used to be quarterback," you tell him.

"We've already got Brady Sanchez playing there. But we'll see how it all fits at practice. Coach Martin will get you some pads."

You quickly put on your gear and run onto the field. Yes, you're back!

"Run a lap and then pick a drill," Coach Louis says.

You run the circumference of the field, smiling as you pass each goal post. It feels good to be here, packed into pads, head in a helmet.

At the end of the run, you look to the middle. The rest of the team is divided into two groups. One is doing some running drills. The other group is catching and throwing. The coach said to pick a drill. What will you choose to do?

To choose the running drills, go to page 74.

To choose the throwing drills, go to page 75.

At the end of practice, Coach Louis calls you over to him. "I'll tell you what, Jesse: You sure are a well-rounded player. I think I could put you at just about any position on this team."

You blush, but you feel proud for working so hard.

"You said you want to be quarterback, but I like you at wide receiver. We could really use you there."

"Sure, Coach."

"Good." He smiles. "Our first game is this weekend. Learn the playbook by then, and I'll get you onto the field. See you tomorrow."

As you jog toward the locker room, you glance to your right. The team's kicker boots a 35-yard field goal straight through the goal posts. He slaps hands with a teammate, and then he takes off his helmet.

Wait . . . what?

Long, straight light-brown hair falls just below the kicker's shoulders. All of that hair was crammed inside his helmet. No, *her* helmet.

You recognize the kicker at once: Briley Temple. You met her in preschool and have been friends ever since. She was always a star soccer player, so you're surprised to see her here. Maybe the coaches couldn't find anyone else who could do the job.

You wait for her.

She squints her eyes as she gets closer to you. Then she stops, and her eyes widen. "Jesse Allan?"

You smile. "Yeah, that's me."

She moves a couple steps closer. "What are you doing here?" she asks.

"Playing football. What are you doing here?"

"The same," she answers. "You were gone awhile."

"Yep."

Awkward silence.

"Okay, I guess you'll make me ask," she finally says. "Where have you been?"

From the day you met her, you've trusted Briley. You don't think you've ever lied to her. But this might be the time to start. You didn't tell the other players the truth. If you tell her and word gets out, well, things could get awkward with your teammates. Still, it would be nice to tell someone about your life as a runaway. Maybe Briley could help you adjust to this new life with your uncle. What will you choose to do?

To change the subject, go to page 44.

To tell the truth, go to page 61.

Uncle Gary has always been good to you. You decide to trust him. "Yeah, okay, lunch would be nice. Pizza sounds really good."

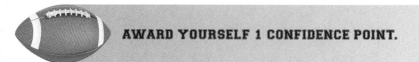

AWARD YOURSELF 1 CONFIDENCE POINT.

Uncle Gary drives you to your favorite restaurant in all of Rosso: Dar's Pizza. Just looking at the menu and smelling pizza in the oven makes you drool.

Go to the next page.

"How are you?" he asks. "Have you been okay? Where are you staying?"

"With friends," you lie.

Uncle Gary smiles. "That's good. And how's school? How are your grades?"

You lie again. "I get mostly Bs and Cs."

His smile fades a little. He scratches his head. "That's odd. I've been checking the schools. More than once. They never had any records of you."

Your gaze drops to the floor.

"If you won't be straight with me, I'll have to guess," he says. He doesn't sound angry. Just sad. "You're home-less. You sleep wherever you can. You eat whatever you find. You don't go to school—I already know that. Did I get anything else wrong?"

You don't look up. You just shake your head.

Uncle Gary doesn't speak for nearly a minute. When he does, it's almost a whisper. "I don't understand. I thought your mom would have set something up—a family, a place to live."

"She did," you answer, "with her cousin. But I didn't want to move to Minnesota. So . . ."

"So you ran away?"

You look at him and nod. "Yeah."

Uncle Gary tries to keep his face even, but you see pain in it. It reminds you of the holiday you spent with him after his wife died. Both of them were so nice. They never had children of their own, so they always found extra time to spend with you.

"What about your friends?" he asks. "What about football? Don't you miss all of that?"

You take a deep breath. "I . . . of course, I do. I mean, I do miss my friends, and I really wish I played football. But that life is behind me now."

This is hard to talk about. You love everything about football: the plays, the hits, the throws, the teammates.

You realize a moment too late that you're about to cry. Tears roll down your face before you can blink them away. You jerk your head in the other direction as fast as you can.

Uncle Gary sighs. "I'm sorry."

"It's all right," you say. "I'm glad to have someone to tell. The other relatives wanted me to move to Japan, but that sounded even worse. I don't speak Japanese, and they were practically strangers."

Your uncle stares at you for a long time. Then he nods firmly, as if he's just made a big decision. "Well, Jesse, there's only one thing to do."

Oh, no. Is he going to call social services? Turn you in? Bring you to Minnesota? Make you move to Japan?

You slowly slide to the edge of your seat. You'll make a run for it if you have to.

"I think you should move in with me," he says.

You don't run, but you almost fall out of your seat.

Uncle Gary is family, but you don't really know him, not anymore. Is agreeing to live with him a good idea? Or are you better off on your own? What will you choose to do?

To live with Uncle Gary, go to page 32.

To turn down his offer, go to page 12.

You're thinking too much. The coach knows what's best. You'll run his play. "28! 9! 28!" you shout.

Nick Helton snaps the ball, and everyone on your team springs into action. You scoot back and hold the ball out for Connor Justin, the team's best running back. He pretends to take it from you.

You tuck the ball against your body and sprint for the goal line. A big linebacker stands in your path, but wide receiver Brady Sanchez blocks him, knocking him out of the way.

The path is open. You're going to score. You're going to win!

Someone hits you hard on your right side. Your feet leave the ground, and you find yourself flying sideways. You twist, extend your arms, and reach forward with the ball.

You land on your stomach with a thud, and you look at the football hopefully. It's still in your hand . . . just inches short of the end zone.

A referee blows his whistle, and the play is over.

It doesn't matter how close you are. You've lost the championship game.

Go to page 28.

Briley was never quiet or shy, but that didn't mean she couldn't keep a secret. You do remember that Briley was a good friend.

You step closer to her. "I need you to keep this quiet, okay?" you whisper.

"Of course."

"I told the guys something different."

"Got it."

You take a deep breath. "After my dad left us and my mom died, I was supposed to move to Japan."

"All the way over there? Is that where you've been?"

"No, my mom had a cousin in Minnesota."

"Well, that's closer. Colder, but closer."

"I didn't want to move there, either . . . so I ran away. I've been living on the street for the past year."

AWARD YOURSELF 1 TEAMWORK POINT.

You don't remember ever seeing Briley speechless. But her mouth hangs open. She stares at you, her face frozen in surprise.

You continue. "Last week, my uncle found me. I moved in with him."

Her mouth remains open, but at least she blinks.

"So, here I am."

She closes her mouth and nods. "So, here you are."

Go to page 45.

Your game against Canton was not a good one, but you've been doing much better at practice this week. However, almost all of your experience has come from playing quarterback. It feels like the position you were born to play.

Plus, the backup quarterback holds the football for the kicker during extra points and field goals. That means extra time with Briley every day during practice. It surprises you how happy that makes you feel. Your cheeks grow warm as you think about it. Hopefully, Coach doesn't notice.

"I'd like to improve my game at wide receiver," you tell him. "But I know a lot more about quarterback. I think I'll be a better help to the team if I move over to that position."

"Good answer, Jesse. You're officially the backup QB. But I still plan to use you at wide receiver when the need arises—so keep practicing those catches, too."

AWARD YOURSELF 1 TEAMWORK POINT.

Go to the next page.

Four nights later, the Gators are up against the Homerville Hawks. You find that being the backup quarterback is easy—and hard. You feel relaxed because you probably won't play. But you also feel left out, disconnected from the game.

On the Gators' first possession, Brady marches down the field, mixing in passes and runs. He even scampers for 21 yards to get the ball down to the 18-yard line. On the next play, Connor Justin takes the handoff, breaks a tackle at the line of scrimmage, then sprints to the end zone. Touchdown!

The Hawks are a good team, though. They respond with a long drive of their own. They keep the football for more than seven minutes on their way to a tying touchdown run.

"Defense!" Coach Louis yells. "Get your heads screwed back on!"

Both defenses do just that for the rest of the half. Neither team is able to get past midfield, and the game enters halftime in a 7–7 tie.

In the locker room, Coach asks the team, "What are you doing out there? Do you remember what we've done in practice? I want you to get out there for the second half and show me that we're not all wasting our time every day!"

Connor breaks the tie in the third quarter. He scores his second touchdown of the day—this one on a 42-yard burst.

But again the Hawks respond. Their quarterback completes only his third pass of the game, but it's an 80-yard bomb to a speedy receiver. After the extra point, the game is knotted up again, 14–14.

On the Gators' next possession, Brady drops back to pass and is smashed by two defensive players. It was a good play by the defense, but Brady is slow to get up. When he finally does stand, his legs seem a bit wobbly.

"Jesse!" Coach yells.

You grab your helmet. "Yeah, Coach?"

"Get in there for Brady."

You jog onto the field as the starting quarterback limps off. You have no idea if you'll be in for one play or the rest of the game, but your arms tingle with excitement. Your heart is pumping. Your mind is sharp. You're ready to win this game.

After Brady's sack, it's third down and 13 yards to go. Nick snaps the football to you, and your team springs into motion. Your offensive linemen keep the defense away from you, as your receivers work to get open. You roll a few steps to your right, and Michael flashes open between the two safeties. You don't think.

You just throw. The ball spirals 22 yards across the field—and right into his hands. He's tackled there, but that's a first down for the Gators!

It's the only pass you throw for the rest of the drive. You hand off on five straight plays, and Connor scores his third touchdown of the game! Briley's extra point is blocked, but the Gators now lead, 20–14.

Both defenses play strong through the rest of the third quarter and into the fourth. With five minutes to play, the Hawks break into the end zone. Their kicker blasts the ball through the uprights. The extra point is good—which is not good news for you. The Hawks now lead, 21–20.

You look into the stands. Your uncle is there, in the same spot as last time, with Tina. That touchdown probably caused his back to straighten a bit.

After the kickoff, you run to the huddle, tell your team the play, and jog to the line of scrimmage. You can feel the pressure of the game, but you don't have butterflies in your stomach. You've been in this kind of game before. You settle in to playing just like you used to, and you drive the Gators, pass after pass, down to the 34-yard line.

On third down, with four yards to go, Coach signals for a pass play.

Nick snaps the ball, and Kyle runs open down the sideline. You heave the football toward the front corner of the end zone. Kyle and the ball arrive at the same spot at the same time. He leaps into the air, falls to the ground, and the referee signals him down at the one-yard line.

Coach calls for a running play to Connor. From here, it should be easy to get his fourth touchdown. But on the next play, Nick snaps the football too soon. The defense breaks through the line before your blockers are ready to stop them.

You need to make a decision, and you need to do so quickly. Should you stick with the play and pitch the ball to Connor? Or should you keep it and run with it yourself? What will you choose to do?

To pitch the ball, go to page 100.

To keep the ball, go to page 26.

A lot has changed in the past couple of days. You're a bit stressed out. You need a long weekend to get used to your uncle and your new home.

"Yeah, I think I'll stay here. It would be good for you to call the school. Thanks, Uncle Gary."

If you could get back out on the football field, that would help, too. You didn't realize how much you missed it until it was offered again.

After your uncle leaves for work, you decide to walk to the field. You want to step on the grass, run, stand in the end zone.

When you arrive, a gym class is there, learning the game. So much for that idea.

You go to the community center, instead. You try to workout on some of the equipment, but you feel tired and weak. All of that time on the street—without much exercise or food—has you way out of football shape. Still, you try to lift weights for a while, but you soon decide to wait until you're stronger and healthier.

Go to the next page.

On Saturday, Uncle Gary takes you shopping for some new clothes. You also meet his girlfriend, Tina. On Sunday afternoon, she helps you paint your room green, black, and white. Those are the colors of your football team, the Rosso Gators.

When Monday morning comes, your stomach feels tight, like stitches are pinching it together. Uncle Gary promises to drop off your football paperwork. If it weren't for football, you're not sure you'd feel brave enough to go back to school at all.

You make it through the morning okay. At lunchtime, someone calls your name in the cafeteria. You look toward the voice and see Santiago Ramirez. You two have played football together since you were 10 years old. He was always bigger than you, and he was a good blocker on the offensive line—he probably still is.

He waves you over. "Jesse, sit over here."

You do as he asks and are quickly joined by several other players on the team.

"Dude, where have you been?" Santiago asks. "We missed you."

You do not want to go into that right now. What would these people think of you? You have done some things that you're not proud of—like stealing food to eat. You have to tell them something, though. Two ideas pop into your head. You can tell them you've been homeschooling. That sounds okay. Or you can tell them you've been living with your mom's family in Japan. They'd think that was really cool. What will you choose to do?

To say you were homeschooling, go to page 51.

To say you were in Japan, go to page 14.

You shake your head. "No, thanks, I already ate." It isn't a lie, but you don't mention how hungry you are.

Uncle Gary shrugs. "Okay, I can wait to eat. Let's talk right here." He sits down beside you.

Darn, if you still have to talk to him, maybe you should've said yes to the pizza.

Go to page 57.

You're angry, and you have every right to be. That was an illegal play, and it was against your friend. You haven't had very many friends in recent months, but you know that they should stick up for each other—no matter what.

The dirty Coyote tries to walk away, but some of your teammates have noticed him. They start to block his path. It's time to prove that you're one of them. It's time to take care of this bully.

You step behind him and push him. He stumbles and turns.

"What the—?" he starts to say.

"You tackled our kicker."

"Get over it. She's not dead," he sneers.

The word "dead" instantly brings a memory of your mom. It's suddenly as if he didn't just hit Briley; he's making fun of your mom. Anger roars within you.

Go to the next page.

For a moment, everything looks red. Then you push the kid to the ground and leap on top of him. Your fists fly against his head, but you can't hurt him. He's wearing a helmet.

One of his teammates tackles you. One of yours tackles him. A moment later, everyone on the field is fighting.

You hear the referees' whistles blasting, over and over again. Then you feel a strong arm pull you away from the other players. You make a fist with your hand and spin, ready to punch.

You don't see a Coyote, though. It's Coach Louis.

"Look what you started, Jesse. You're not the person I thought you were. Go to the locker room and get out of that football gear. You're off the team."

You should say something. You should apologize or make an excuse—anything. But no words come to you. You blew your chance, and you know it's too late to take back what you've done.

Go to page 79.

You hustle to the group that's running. You need to get into shape, and running is a great way to do it.

Coach Martin leads the team in a drill called "Plant and Cut." You get in line and watch how it's done: run with the ball in a diagonal, plant your outside foot, and cut in the other direction.

You've always loved running. You used to go to the track and run with your mom. She was a track runner back when she was in high school. She participated in local races for fun . . . until she got sick.

The thought of your mom brings on a twinge of sadness, but she'd be proud to see you now. You got your quickness from her.

 **AWARD YOURSELF 2 SPEED POINTS.**

Go to page 54.

You hustle to the group that's catching and throwing footballs. Coach Louis leads the team in a drill called "Four Cone Distraction."

You get in line and watch how it's done: catch the football as you're standing between four cones, while a defender distracts you by waving his hands in your face. Everyone also takes turns throwing. No problem.

You've always loved catching and throwing. Any ball. You used to play catch with your dad a lot. He was a football player back when he was in high school. He also played basketball and baseball. Dad still participated in a few local leagues for fun . . . until he left.

The thought of your dad brings on a twinge of sadness, but he'd be proud to see you now. You got your football skills from him.

AWARD YOURSELF 2 SKILL POINTS.

Go to page 54.

You won't talk to your teacher. It's her job to help students, and she'll think that's more important than football. And maybe she's right, but for now, football feels like the only reason you're here.

"I'm sorry," you tell her. "I didn't have time to get it done. I'm still adjusting to my new schedule. Is it okay if I turn it in later?"

"I'll accept that excuse, this once, Jesse. But from now on, I expect the same from you as everyone. How about you turn it in tomorrow?" Mrs. Meyer says. It isn't a question.

"Sure," you agree.

By the end of the day, you're more frustrated than you were on Friday. The writing homework keeps piling up—in every class.

You wait for Briley, hoping she can help. But that idea starts to sound like a bad one. You don't want her to know you can't write. What will she think of you? You couldn't take it if she laughed.

Instead, you go to the locker room. Brady is there. You two were good friends before you ran away. Maybe he can help.

You sit. "Do you have Mrs. Meyer for English?"

"Yeah."

"Did you do the questions for the first few chapters of *Maniac*?"

"Yes, but they were due today," he says.

"Do you remember the answers?"

"Sure. It was pretty easy," he says.

You rub your hand through your hair. "Listen, this might sound dumb, but do you think you could write them down for me?"

Brady laughs. "You didn't read the book, huh? You should. It's good."

"Um, I will. But can you help me?" you ask.

He smiles. "No problem."

The next day, you turn in your homework—well, the answers Brady wrote for you.

Before you leave class, Mrs. Meyer says, "Can I talk to you for a minute?" She holds up the assignment. "Did you write this?"

If she's asking, she already knows the answer.

"No, but—"

"Someone else did your homework?"

"No, I mean . . . yes, but it's not like that," you start to explain.

"Then how is it, Jesse?" She looks so disappointed.

"I can't wr—" you begin to say. But you change your mind. You're too embarrassed. "Oh, I don't know. It's too much work all at once."

She shakes her head. "Well, Jesse, I'm afraid I have some bad news." Her voice is soft, and it's tinged with sadness. "The school has a strict policy against cheating. I'll have to give you a failing grade, which means you won't be allowed to play football."

The news hits you harder than any defensive end ever could. You run out of her classroom and out of school. You run to Gary's house, pack your backpack, and leave. You don't know where you're going, but it will be as far away from this place as possible.

Go to the next page.

GAME
OVER

TRY AGAIN.

Your game against Canton was not a good one, but you've been doing much better at practice this week. If you change positions now, it would feel a bit like giving up, and you don't want to do that. Besides, the bottom line is that your position doesn't matter too much. You just want to play football.

"I'd like to improve my game at wide receiver," you tell him. "I know a lot more about being a quarterback. But I'll be a better help to the team if I keep working on catching the ball."

"Good answer, Jesse. I can use you at wide receiver. But do me a favor: Learn the plays at quarterback, too. Hopefully, we last the whole season with Brady. However, every football team is one injury away from needing a new quarterback."

"Thanks, Coach, I will."

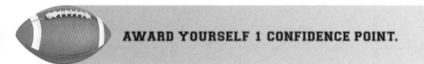 **AWARD YOURSELF 1 CONFIDENCE POINT.**

Go to the next page.

Four nights later, the Gators are up against the Homerville Hawks. You aren't a starter, but you feel nervous and excited because you know you'll get to play. You can make a difference for your team—but, deep down, you're afraid you might drop another pass.

On the Gators' first possession, Brady marches down the field, mixing in passes and runs. He even scampers for 21 yards to get the ball down to the 18-yard line. On the next play, Connor Justin takes the handoff, breaks a tackle at the line of scrimmage, then sprints to the end zone. Touchdown!

The Hawks are a good team, though. They respond with a long drive of their own. They keep the football for more than seven minutes on their way to a tying touchdown run.

"Defense!" Coach Louis yells. "Get your heads screwed back on!"

Both defenses do just that for the rest of the half. Neither team is able to get past midfield, and the game enters halftime with a 7–7 tie.

In the locker room, Coach asks the team, "What are you doing out there? Do you remember what we've done in practice? I want you to get out there for the second half and show me that we're not all wasting our time every day!"

Connor breaks the tie in the third quarter. He scores his second touchdown of the day—this one on a 42-yard run.

But again the Hawks respond. Their quarterback completes only his third pass of the game, but it's an 80-yard bomb to a speedy receiver. After the extra point, the game is knotted up again, 14–14.

On the Gators' next possession, Brady drops back to pass and is smashed by two defensive players. It was a good play by the defense, but Brady is slow to get up. When he finally does stand, his legs seem a bit wobbly.

"Jesse!" Coach yells.

You grab your helmet. "Yeah, Coach?"

"Did you look at those plays at quarterback?"

The question surprises you. "Yeah, I did."

"Then get in there for Brady."

You jog onto the field as the starting quarterback limps off. You have no idea if you'll be in for one play or the rest of the game, but your arms tingle with excitement. Your heart is pumping. Your mind is sharp. You're ready to win this game.

After Brady's sack, it's third down and 13 yards to go. Nick snaps the football to you, and your team springs into motion. Your offensive linemen keep the defense away from you, as your receivers work to get open. You roll a few steps to your right, and Michael flashes open between the two safeties. You don't think. You just throw. The ball spirals 22 yards across the field—and right into his hands. He's tackled there, but that's a first down for the Gators!

It's the only pass you throw for the rest of the drive. You hand off on five straight plays, and Connor scores his third touchdown of the game! Briley's extra point is blocked, but the Gators now lead, 20–14.

Both defenses play strong through the rest of the third quarter and into the fourth. With five minutes to play, the Hawks break into the end zone. Their kicker blasts the ball through the uprights, and the extra point is good—which is not good news for you. The Hawks now lead, 21–20.

You look into the stands. Your uncle is there, in the same spot as last time, with Tina. That touchdown probably caused his back to straighten a bit.

After the kickoff, you run to the huddle, tell your team the play, and jog to the line of scrimmage. You can feel the pressure of the game, but you don't have butterflies in your stomach. You've been in this kind of game before. You settle into playing just like you used to, and you drive the Gators, pass after pass, down to the 34-yard line.

On third down, with four yards to go, Coach signals for a pass play.

Nick snaps the ball, and Kyle runs open down the sideline. You heave the football toward the front corner of the end zone. Kyle and the ball arrive at the same spot at the same time. He leaps into the air, falls to the ground, and the referee signals him down at the one-yard line.

Coach calls for a running play to Connor. From here, it should be easy to get his fourth touchdown. But on the next play, Nick snaps the football too soon. The defense breaks through the line before your blockers are ready to stop them.

You need to make a decision, and you need to do it fast. Should you stick with the play and pitch the ball to Connor? Or should you keep it and run with it yourself? What will you choose to do?

To pitch the ball, go to page 100.

To keep the ball, go to page 26.

Coach signals for a deep pass. In your heart, you know it's impossible, but you have to try.

When Nick snaps the ball, you scan the field. Kyle, Michael, and three other receivers dash to the end zone. Eight Rams are waiting to cover them. Three rushers try to sack you. They're blocked by your linemen.

That leaves a lot of open space between you and the end zone. The defense is so focused on covering a pass that they've left you with room to run.

You take off toward the goal line like a rocket. You put into play everything you know, everything you've learned. You take all the drills from practice, and you channel that speed and that skill into this one play.

The Rams are defending champions. They must have a great coach because they know what to do. The moment you cross the line of scrimmage, every defender in the end zone abandons the receivers—because now you cannot throw to them.

You don't even get to the 10-yard line before a Ram safety tackles you. As the Sugar Valley fans celebrate, you just lie on the grass, wishing you could disappear into it like a drop of rain.

Go to page 79.

You're too angry. You can't do this, not now. You know it might ruin Uncle Gary's evening, but you need to be honest. "No, sorry," you say. "I'm not ready."

Uncle Gary sighs deeply. "I'd be lying if I said I liked that answer, but I understand. We can give you more time."

"We?" The word catches your ear. "You've already talked to him?"

"I called him. I told him I had you. He deserved to know that." Uncle Gary stops for a moment. "I don't know if I should tell you this, but I think it's important. He started to cry, Jesse. I think it's really hard for him to face up to what he did."

The anger inside you becomes too much to hold in. So you let it out. "Good! He left me, and he left Mom! I hope he's miserable!"

Uncle Gary doesn't say anything more. He just nods. He takes the check from the table, and he walks to the register. Eventually, you get up and follow him out.

8

THE PLAYOFFS

At school, you enjoy Mrs. Beverage's class more and more. Yesterday, she had you write about some funny/weird pictures that she found online. The one you wrote about was a man with a camera trying to take a picture of a boa constrictor as it wrapped around his body.

Today, all the students are writing instructions on how to make a peanut butter and jelly sandwich.

"I brought the stuff," she says, "and you get to make the sandwiches." She lifts her finger. "By following your own instructions, of course."

As for football, the Gators finished the regular season with only two losses. That was good enough to make it into the championship bracket of the playoffs. The team won its Round 1 game, 35–7.

You and Brady continue to take turns as Rosso's quarterback. Neither one of you can win the job because you both seem to follow every good game with a not-so-good one.

Tonight is a Round 2 matchup against the Fairmont Bulldogs, and you're still not whether you or Brady is starting. You want to play. The Gators' season is on the line. If you win, you advance to the quarterfinals. If you lose, the season is over.

The game is in Rosso, thankfully. You much prefer playing in front of the Gator fans. Plus, you're used to seeing Uncle Gary and your soon-to-be aunt, Tina, in the bleachers.

You're a bit surprised when Coach says, "Jesse, you're in at quarterback tonight."

Brady has started more games than you, and both of you played well in Round 1. You'll have to step up your play and prove that Coach made the right choice.

You do just that in the first quarter. The Gators aren't able to score, but you play well, helping the team eat up yards on every drive. The defense does its job, too. As the quarter ends, the score is 0–0.

"Brady, I want you in for the second quarter," Coach Louis announces.

Your mouth hangs open. You stare at the coach, and your mind races. *What did I do wrong?*

Coach Louis turns toward you, almost as if he can read your mind. He waves for you to come over to him. "Take a look at the scoreboard, Jesse," he says. "Do you see that zero on our side of the board?"

Your shoulders slump. "Yes, Coach."

"I need more from you," he says. "Your job is to get us points. Now, we'll see what Brady can do."

If the entire Bulldog defense had piled on top of you, it would feel better than this. You walk to the bench and sit next to Briley.

"This stinks," you say.

"At least you've been on the field," she says. "I've been over here the whole game."

"Yeah, according to Coach Louis, that's my fault," you mumble.

Two minutes before halftime, Brady fumbles. A Bulldog defensive end grabs it off the ground and runs for the end zone. No Gator comes close to him; it's an easy touchdown for Fairmont. They add a two-point conversion, and the score stands at 0–8 at halftime.

In the third quarter, you get another chance to play. You have to get points, or you'll be benched—and your Gators might lose.

You move the team down the field, just like you did in the first quarter. You connect on passes to Michael and to Kyle, and you mix in a few handoffs to Connor.

You put together the best offensive drive by either team, guiding the Gators to the eight-yard line.

You drop back to pass and look for Kyle. He sprints five yards into the end zone. Then he spins around and starts running back toward you. He's open, and you zip the ball straight to him.

Touchdown!

Briley kicks the extra point, making it a 7–8 game.

The Gator defense continues to dominate Fairmont's offense. The Bulldogs can't get anything going on the ground or through the air.

Neither can you. Rosso doesn't manage a score for the rest of the third. Lucky for you, the Gators' touchdown seems to be enough for Coach Louis. He leaves you in when the fourth quarter begins.

You glance over at Brady. He looks ready to toss his helmet into the stands. Of course, you know he won't. He's a team player. You'd be upset, too, if you were the one on the bench.

Time winds down. You move the ball across the 50-yard line on every possession. But you can't get close enough for a field goal, let alone a touchdown.

With only 2:27 left to play, you get the football one final time. You complete short passes to Michael and Connor. Then you hit Kyle in the middle of the field for 31 yards.

You sneak in a running play that gains three yards. Then you fire an incomplete pass. On third down, with seven yards to go, Coach Louis calls another pass play.

You take the snap from center and drop back. You glance at Kyle, and then you look over at Michael. Both of them are covered, but you have to make a play. If you throw a perfect pass, you should be able to sneak it past the defender. But should you throw the ball to Kyle or to Michael?

Add together your talent points and your skill points. How many points do you have?

If you have 3 or more points, go to page 142.

If you have 2 or fewer points, go to page 134.

"I want to go out there, I guess." You stand up and follow Gary to the kitchen.

Your dad is talking to Tina. He's lost a lot of weight, and he looks . . . exhausted. You turn away from him, go to the counter, and grab the salad tongs. You mix the salad, although you already did so half an hour ago.

"Hey, Jesse." Your dad sounds just like his brother.

You don't turn from the counter. "Hey."

"I hear your football team made it to the semifinals. Congratulations"

You nod. "Thanks."

Total silence.

Uncle Gary starts to say something, but your dad interrupts him. "Jesse, I'm so sorry—."

You run from the kitchen, grab a picture of your mom, and run back to the kitchen. You hold it up for your dad. "You left us!"

"I . . . I couldn't . . ." He looks down. When he lifts his head again, he says, "I took that picture of you and your mom. We went for a picnic at the park. You loved being outside."

"Do you know I lived outside for a year?" you ask, making it sound like an accusation.

He looks down again and nods.

"Because you left," you say, "and Mom died?"

He doesn't look up. "I never knew she was sick. Gary's the one who told me . . . after she passed away." He wipes his cheeks. "I'm so—" He chokes, tries again. "I'm so sorry."

"I'm hungry," you say. "Can we eat?"

"Of course," Tina answers.

Tina hands out the plates. Everyone gets their food and sits at the table.

You don't say anything, just eat and listen to your uncle and your dad talk about their jobs. The topic shifts to Gary and Tina's wedding, and there's even a bit of laughter—from everyone except you.

AWARD YOURSELF 1 TEAMWORK POINT.

Go to the next page.

The semifinal game has you matched up against the Calhoun Raiders, a team you've never played before.

"They got this far because they're an excellent team," says Coach. "But you guys have been strong all season. I know you can win."

Your thoughts shift to last Sunday, when your dad asked if he could come to the game. You told him yes. What else could you say?

When you run out to the field for warm-ups, you see Tina and Gary watching from the stands. Your dad is there, too. As upset as you feel, part of you is glad that he's here. It kind of feels like old times.

Coach Louis chooses you to start the game, and you feel energy pulse through your body. You are ready to win this game!

That positive feeling quickly turns to frustration. The Gator offense starts slowly.

In the second quarter, the score remains tied at zero. You know that Coach is going to replace you with Brady. It will be so embarrassing in front of your dad. He remembers you as a star player—not someone who gets benched. But Coach yells your name, and you run onto the field. Now, you can remind your dad of the football player you used to be.

Except things don't turn out like you hope.

You throw a pass to Kyle, but a Raider safety reads the play. He jumps in front of the throw and intercepts the football. He streaks down the sideline, all the way to the end zone.

You avoid looking at your dad as you head for the bench. You try to convince yourself that this is normal, that even the best quarterbacks make mistakes. But to do this in front of your father? You probably won't see the field for the rest of the game . . .

Brady doesn't exactly light up the scoreboard, either. The score remains 0–7 until the middle of the third quarter. That's when Brady gets sacked—hard.

He gets up holding his wrist. When the team trainer tries to move it, he cries out in pain. That's not good.

"Jesse, you're in," Coach says. He doesn't look happy. His face shows plenty of doubt.

Play after play, things start to go right. You march the team down the field and end the drive with a plunge into the end zone. Touchdown!

The fourth quarter comes, and neither Calhoun nor Rosso can gain an advantage. The game remains tied, 7–7, as both teams battle back and forth.

With two minutes to play, Coach Louis calls the team together. "We've done it before, and we'll do it again. Let's get out there and win this!"

You pass to Michael for a gain of 12. You pass to Kyle, and he moves the football into Raiders' territory. Play by play, you lead the Gators to the eight-yard line.

Nick snaps the ball; you look for Michael in the end zone. Two defensive backs cover him. Kyle is blanketed, too. If you wait for a second, he might get open. But if you wait too long, you will get sacked. Do you have time? Or should you throw the football out of bounds?

How many confidence points do you have?

If you have 3 or more points, go to page 131.

If you have 2 or fewer points, go to page 111.

"Brady, I'm worried about your injury. Are you sure you're okay?" you ask.

He nods. "I'm fine. I can win this for us."

You shrug. "Okay, I get it. I've been gone a year, and this is your team now. If you're all right to play, get out there and win."

You slap him on the back, and the two of you walk onto the field together.

AWARD YOURSELF 1 TEAMWORK POINT.

The Eagles score again to start the third quarter: The kicker hits a field goal from the 15-yard line, making it a 0–17 game.

Brady answers. He connects on a pass to the tight end for 16 yards. Then he runs the same play again, and it goes for 11. Two plays later, Connor takes the hand-off, squirts through the line, and dashes 50 yards for a touchdown! But the celebration doesn't last long. Brady is on the ground back at the 50, and he isn't getting up.

The coaches and trainers rush out to him. They are soon able to help him up, and he hops off the field.

Uh, oh, it looks like he hurt his foot again.

When play continues, Briley kicks the extra point, making the score 7–17.

The Gators' first score of the night seems to wake up the defense. Truc forces a fumble and recovers the ball on the Eagles' 24-yard line.

This time, you lead the offense onto the field.

Coach Louis calls a pass play to Kyle, but he can't get open. You look toward Michael; he's covered too. There's nowhere to throw the ball, and your linemen can't block forever. You know what to do: run.

You dodge a tackle, break free from a linebacker who grabs your jersey, and dive across the goal line.

Touchdown!

You jump off the ground and run to every teammate on the field, slapping high-fives and yelling excitedly. You glance at your uncle; he's clapping and cheering.

You force yourself to settle down. The game's not over, and the Gators are still down by three.

Rosso's defense again gets the job done. Valdosta doesn't make it past the 40-yard line. They punt the ball to your team, and you move deep into the Eagles' end of the field.

When it's first down on the 18-yard line, Coach calls for a pass to Michael in the end zone. You fake a run to Connor. Then you pump the ball toward Kyle, like you're going to throw it. The defense falls for it, and Michael stands wide open. You throw one of your best passes of the night . . . touchdown!

The clock runs out on the Eagles before they reach midfield. The Rosso Gators win!

Go to page 148.

Your coach called the play. Even though the center made a mistake, you must trust your team to execute it. You pitch the football to Connor.

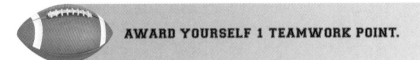

AWARD YOURSELF 1 TEAMWORK POINT.

Three defensive players surround him, but he spins and runs back toward you. As he passes by, you launch yourself at the defenders—and you block two of them at once.

Connor cuts left and gets by another defender, but he trips. He stumbles . . . regains his balance, and runs into the end zone. The Gators lead, 26–21!

The fans roar in celebration, but there are still two minutes to go. That can be a long time in a game.

The defense plays tough. They sack the quarterback and force a fumble. A mix of defensive and offensive linemen pile on top of it. When the referees sort out the players, Truc is holding the football.

The Gators win again!

6

SCHOOL MEETING

On Monday morning, Uncle Gary puts a slice of egg bake on your plate.

"Have you ever thought of being a chef?" you ask.

"Actually, I was interested a few years back," he says. "But the best jobs are in New York. I didn't want to leave Rosso."

You stop your fork midway between your plate and mouth. "You never wanted to leave Rosso?"

"Your Aunt Karyn and I were settled here. I decided that cooking would be a hobby."

You nod and keep eating. Every bite is delicious.

"Jesse, I forgot to mention that I've got a meeting at school today."

Suddenly, the food doesn't taste as good. You can guess what's coming next.

"Your teachers say you can't write."

You look down at your egg bake. Your brain feels just as scrambled as those eggs.

For what feels like an hour, no one says a word. But, finally, Uncle Gary asks, "Is it true?"

Again, there's silence. He's waiting for an answer.

"Yeah." Your cheeks grow warm. You refuse to look at him.

Quietly, he says, "You could have told me."

You nod.

He tries to make his voice sound cheerful. "We'll get it figured out."

That's easy for him to say.

At practice, you have a hard time focusing. You want to know what the teachers told your uncle.

When he picks you up, you don't even close the car door before you say, "How was the meeting?"

"Well," he replies, "I'll be honest. Your teachers are worried because of the differences in what you can and can't do. For example, you're really good at math but struggle to write word problems."

"They're the worst."

"Your English teacher had the most to say. That's another odd difference: You're a great reader, but . . ."

"Right."

"So you're going to get tested next week to see what's going on. Then I'll meet with them to talk about the next steps."

You lean your head back against your seat. Test then next steps? You can work with that.

The tests take up most of your afternoon, but you're finished in time for practice. Since you are now the "official" backup quarterback, you hold the football for the kicker. That means you get to spend more time with Briley. It's your favorite part of practice. She makes you laugh every single day.

On Friday, your uncle is invited back to school to talk about the test results. You had hoped this wouldn't happen on game day, so you tell Gary not to talk to you about it until after the game.

Your classes still drive you crazy. Writing is so hard; it makes each hour feel like it's moving in slow motion. You don't understand why your brain won't work for you like it does for everyone else. You can't help but wonder why you aren't as smart as your mom or dad were. Of course, you're not so sure anymore about your dad's level of intelligence. It was pretty dumb to leave you and Mom.

After school, Uncle Gary picks you up. At first, you don't say anything, but the silence is too much to bear.

"You got the results?" you ask.

"You didn't want to talk about it before the game. Remember? I'll tell you if you want, but it can wait."

What's better? Knowing or not knowing? If you don't know, will you be too curious to concentrate on football? Or if you do know, will any bad news shatter your confidence? Should you find out now or after the game? What will you choose to do?

To find out now, go to page 116.

To wait until later, go to page 128.

You turn and look at Briley. She reaches down and helps you to your feet, which works to calm you.

You shout to your linemen, "Come on, come on," and you motion them over to you.

When they get close, you hook elbows with Santiago and Briley. Your other teammates hook elbows, too. Secured into a human chain, you march off the field together, showing the Coyotes—and the dirty player—what a *real* team looks like.

When you reach the sideline, Coach pulls you aside. "I saw that, Jesse. You handled it like a pro." He looks up at the scoreboard. "Let's give you another try at QB. Get in there on our next drive."

Perhaps they are inspired by your show of teamwork; the defense suddenly plays on fire. The Coyote offense can't get anything going.

When the fourth quarter begins, you start to chip away, gaining first downs while eating up the clock. You hit Kyle with a pass, and he carries a Canton safety all the way to the two-yard line. On the very next play, you keep the ball and run it in for a score!

Down 15–17, your team must go for a two-point conversion to tie the game. You handoff to Connor, and he dives across the goal line! It's 17–17.

The Gator defense again prevents the Coyotes from scoring. With under three minutes left, they punt the ball away.

On your first play, you hand the ball to Connor, and he bursts through the defensive unit for 12 yards. You complete a pass for eight yards. Then Kyle snags one and runs for 23 yards.

Time continues to tick away.

Connor makes another great run. Then, on your next pass attempt, you wind up scrambling all the way to the 19-yard line.

"Time out!" you yell to the nearest referee.

There are only nine seconds left.

Briley trots onto the field for her fourth field goal attempt. If she's nervous, she doesn't show it.

You take your spot as holder. Then you look at her. "Are you ready?"

"Ready," she replies calmly.

The snap comes . . . the kick goes up . . . and the Rosso Gators advance to the semifinals!

9

FAMILY REUNION

Since it's Saturday, Gary is home, building Tina a wedding present: a wooden clock. He takes a break for lunch and warms up some leftover lasagna.

"Jesse," your uncle says, "I know you have a lot on your mind right now, but . . . I talked to your dad again. He really wants to see you, soon. I need to ask if you think you're ready? It's football season, and things are pretty busy. But it would mean the world to him."

You swirl a small noodle around with the fork. "I guess," you finally reply.

"I know it'll be weird at first, but . . ."

You know: You have to face up to it. He's your dad, and your mom is gone.

"Maybe tomorrow for lunch?" you suggest.

Gary smiles and nods excitedly. "I think that will work. I'll call him this afternoon."

After lunch, you get out some magazines that Mrs. Beverage gave you for a collage you're creating. As you cut out pictures, you think about your dad, how you'll be seeing him for the first time in years. You don't know how to feel about that. Nervous? Excited? Angry? Afraid? Maybe he'll just disappoint you again and not even bother to show up. You'll find out soon enough.

Sunday morning, you wake up early to help Gary clean the house. You might as well because you're not sure you ever fell asleep. When the place is spotless, you manage to finish some math homework. You can't sit still, so you go for a jog.

Later, after a quick shower, you help Uncle Gary get lunch ready. You make garlic mashed potatoes, and Gary grills steaks.

The food looks and smells delicious, but you feel like throwing up. You almost tell Uncle Gary to cancel your dad's visit, but you know it's too late.

How long has it been? Two years? Three? And you're still angry.

The knock on the door drops your stomach straight to your toes. Without thinking, you run to your bedroom and close the door. You pace back and forth. You hear voices, but they're too low to pick up any words.

There's a knock on your bedroom door.

"Jesse?" It's Uncle Gary. "Can I come in?"

You try to say, "Yes," but it gets stuck in your throat. You open the door.

Gary steps in and closes it behind him. "If you're not ready," he says, "your dad has offered to leave."

You sit on your bed and stare at the frame beside it: a picture of your mom holding you when you were a baby. You remember a Japanese proverb that she used to quote: "The bamboo that bends is stronger than the oak that resists."

"It's okay," you tell Uncle Gary, "I'll see him."

He pats your knee. "Do you want to see him in here, in private? Or would you like to come out and be with Tina and me, too?"

What will you choose to do?

To see your dad in private, go to page 140.

To see your dad with Gary, go to page 92.

Yes, you have your uncle, and it sounds like you'll soon have a new aunt. But a dad is a dad.

"Okay, I'll see him," you say.

Uncle Gary's smile comes back. "I'm so glad, Jesse. I know he'll be happy to hear it."

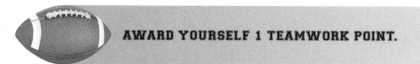

AWARD YOURSELF 1 TEAMWORK POINT.

"You've already talked to him?" you ask.

"I called him. I told him I had you. He deserved to know that." Uncle Gary stops for a moment. "I don't know if I should tell you this, but I think it's important. He started to cry, Jesse. I think it's really hard for him to face up to what he did. But he said he wants to see you. I'll talk to him again, and we'll try to get something set up. It might be a while before that happens, though."

You shrug. "That's okay. I need time, too. He left me, and he left Mom. It's kind of hard to get over."

Uncle Gary doesn't say anything more. He just nods. He takes the check and walks to the register.

Go to page 87.

You trust your offensive line, and you believe in your wide receivers. But you're not sure what to do.

You look left; no one's open. You glance right; your teammates are covered. You scan the middle of the field. One second, two seconds, three seconds . . .

At last, Michael fakes left and zooms right, and he cuts into open field. Instincts take over, and you pull back your arm, getting ready to throw.

At that moment, a terrible force blasts into you from behind. The football pops out of your hand. Your brain registers what happened: The defensive end just sacked you, and you fumbled the football.

As quickly as you can, you roll over and reach for the loose ball. But just before you can snag it, another Raider defender dives on top of it.

The referee blows his whistle and runs straight for the football. He waves his hands in the air and then points in the other direction. "That's the Raiders' ball," he yells. "First down, Raiders!"

This is not the way you wanted to end your season. It's not the way you wanted your dad to see you play. You made a bad choice, and the Gators' season is over.

Go to page 79.

You're not surprised he's asking, but he's still the guy who abandoned you and Mom. He's still a big reason why you ended up as a runaway. He needs to build back your trust, and he hasn't done so yet.

"Uh, Dad . . . I know it's not what you want to hear, but I'm not ready. You can't expect me to just forgive and forget what you did to us."

He doesn't respond, but he grips the steering wheel like he's about to throw it. You look away from him and stare out your window.

A sound comes from him that you don't remember hearing ever before. It sounds like he's choking.

You turn. He's shaking badly and his face is red. But he isn't choking. He's sobbing.

"I . . . messed up . . . bad!"

He wipes his eyes with his sleeve, but the tears are coming so fast. How can he even see?

He looks at you. "I'm sorry, Jesse."

You feel the car drifting, and you glance back out the window. You're in the wrong lane of traffic.

"Dad!"

He jerks the steering wheel to avoid hitting a car. You hear a screech, a honk, and then sounds of thunder.

The car spins. And rolls. And stops, upside down.

Everything goes horribly silent. Your entire body aches. No, *aches* isn't right. Your body feels like it's on fire. There's so much pain in so many places that you can't tell where you're hurt.

You notice your right wrist at an angle you didn't think was possible. You see a hunk of metal sticking into your leg. All you can do now is close your eyes and wait for the sound of sirens.

Go to page 79.

When the other team makes a mistake, a good player takes advantage of it. You spin forward, dart toward the hole, and dive into the end zone for a touchdown!

AWARD YOURSELF 1 SPEED POINT.

Briley kicks in her second extra point of the game, giving you a 14–13 lead.

The back and forth of the final quarter leans in the Falcons' favor. Coach yells at the defense to hold them. But it does little good. The Falcons eventually kick a field goal with just 43 seconds left. That puts the Gators behind, 14–16.

Of course, when there's still time on the clock, there's still hope. You trot onto the field, ready to move your team as quickly as you can.

You complete one pass. Then another. And another. You get all the way to the Falcons' 46-yard line. But there are just three seconds left on the clock—time for one last play. It's too far for a field goal. Your only chance is to heave a long pass into the end zone.

You don't get the opportunity. One of the defensive linemen pushes his way through and sacks you before you can throw the ball.

Game over. You really wanted this win. You wanted to show Coach Louis that you should be starting at QB.

Go to page 137.

If you can't focus on football, you won't play well. You owe it to your team to be at your best. You need to know now. You can handle the news, good or bad.

"Tell me," you say.

He pulls into the driveway of the house and shuts off the car. "Are you sure?" he asks.

You nod. "Go for it."

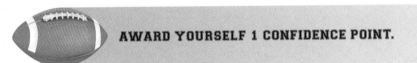

AWARD YOURSELF 1 CONFIDENCE POINT.

"You have a condition called dysgraphia."

"Dyslexia?" you say. "I've heard of that."

Uncle Gary shakes his head. "No, it's dysgraphia."

The word is new to you, so you try to sound it out. You want to understand. "Dis-graff-ee-uh?"

"Right, dysgraphia. Basically, *dys* means bad, and *graphia* means writing."

You frown. "So I write badly. That's it?"

Your uncle pats your shoulder. "No, that's not it. This is good news, Jesse. It's a condition, sort of like a disease. And there's a treatment for it. You can get better. The teachers said it's more common than we might think."

You feel relieved to know what's wrong, but you also feel embarrassed—and mad. Why are you the one with a messed-up brain? Your parents' brains were perfect. Well, your mom's was.

Uncle Gary continues. "You'll work with a new teacher. She will help you get through this."

You appreciate Gary. He tries so hard to make you feel better. Oh, well, at least one thing is for sure: Dysgraphia won't get in the way of playing football.

Go to the next page.

Tonight's game against the Valdosta Eagles is going to be tough. They have skilled players and a rock-solid defense. The Gators will need to play really well to win.

Brady has been okayed by his doctor to start, so you're back to second string.

You only get in for three plays in the first quarter. In part, it's because the Eagles' defense is so tough. But also, the offense doesn't get a single first down. Brady limps in and out of the huddle. He misses a few wide open throws—and the Eagles start crowding the line of scrimmage to stuff the run.

Luckily, your team is playing better on defense. The Eagles put together a few good drives, but they never manage to score any points.

Half of the second quarter passes, and your defense starts to look tired. They allow Valdosta to march all the way down the field, not once but twice. The Eagles pull ahead by a score of 14–0.

Meanwhile, Brady continues to struggle. He nearly trips every time he hands off the ball, and his throws miss by as much as 10 yards. You can tell that his injury is bothering him—and his confidence is shaken.

"Jesse!" Coach Louis yells. "Can you do a better job out there?"

"Yes, Coach," you answer.

"Then go in for Brady and prove it," he says.

Four minutes remain in the first half. The Gators are on the 44-yard line. You call a running play in the huddle and then line up the team.

Connor gains two yards on first down. You get tackled for a loss of three yards on the next play. That makes it third down and 11 yards to go.

Coach signals for a pass play. When the football is snapped to you, you scurry back seven steps. You look toward Kyle, but he's covered by two Eagles. Your eyes shift focus to the other side of the field. Michael is wide open.

You spin a perfect pass straight toward the numbers on his chest. That's when you see the Eagle safety step in front of him. Where did he come from?

It doesn't matter; it's too late. He intercepts the pass, and Michael tackles him from behind.

Thankfully, Valdosta doesn't take advantage of your mistake. Halftime arrives with the score still 0–14.

In the locker room, the coach barks and yells. You imagine the walls vibrating from all of that noise.

As the rest of the team exits, Coach Louis tells you and Brady to stay behind. He snaps, "I can't decide which of you to play, so you two can figure it out. You have five minutes to choose our quarterback."

You watch Coach Louis leave the locker room, your mouth hanging open. Then you look at Brady. He wears the same expression of nervous confusion that you feel on your own face.

The wall clock beside you ticks; every second sounds like the marching band's loud bass drum.

"Dude," Brady says, "I'm the starting QB."

"You're hurt," you reply. "You're not exactly playing your best tonight."

"You threw the interception," he hisses. "Not me."

This is awkward. You don't want to start a fight, but you also want to play. Should you let him go back out there to avoid any trouble? Or should you demand that he lets you play? What will you choose to do?

To let him be quarterback, go to page 97.

To be the quarterback, go to page 146.

You're not surprised he's asking. As soon as you let him back into your life, you knew this day would come. It's sooner than expected, but it feels like a good first step.

"Yes," you say, "good idea. Let's give it a try."

Your dad smacks the steering wheel. "Well, hot dog! That's great, Jesse, just great."

He smiles all the way to Uncle Gary's house, but you're not quite sure how to feel. You'll have to think about it more—once the championship game is over.

10
STATE CHAMPIONSHIP

This is it: the championship game against the Sugar Valley Rams.

Coach Louis makes sure you know that they are a tough opponent. "This team is the defending champion. Not one of you can afford to have an off night. Not one of you can take off even one second of one play. Every single one of you has to be on your game for all four quarters. Do you understand?"

"Yes, Coach!" everyone yells.

The players run onto the field.

Coach calls you back. "It's been an up and down season for you, Jesse. Maybe it hasn't been fair to keep flip-flopping you and Brady. But I do know one thing:

It's made both of you better players. And maybe it's taken the entire season, but you've made a believer out of me. So, tonight, you're my guy, Jesse. Win or lose, good or bad, you're our QB from start to finish. Now, get out there and win this!"

You feel a burst of energy. Goose pimples form on your arms. Coach believes in you, and you're going to show him that he's right.

You chase your teammates onto the field, and you're met by an explosion of cheers. You stop for a moment and scan the stadium. There isn't an empty seat anywhere to be seen. You spot Uncle Gary, Tina, and Dad. They wave and pump their fists.

"Let's do this," you say to yourself.

The Rams win the coin toss, so the Gator defense takes the field first. Thanks in large part to a 40-yard run by the Rams' quarterback, they kick a field goal and gain an early lead.

Your offense responds. Your linemen are among the best in the state, and they prove it on your first drive. The Gators storm into Rams' territory, then all the way down to the six-yard line. Connor runs it into the end zone from there. Rosso leads, 7–3.

The Gators' defense again takes the field. This time, they don't slip up. The Rams are forced to punt.

Neither offense is able to get on track again for the rest of the quarter—or the rest of the half. At halftime, the score of 7–3 still lights up the scoreboard.

The third quarter begins with a Gators' possession. Your drive starts well, and you advance to the 46-yard line. You hand the ball to Connor, and he takes off. But a Rams' linebacker hits him from behind and knocks the football out of his hand.

The Rams recover the fumble.

Two minutes later, Sugar Valley turns that turnover into a touchdown. They regain the lead.

On the sideline, Coach Louis announces, "It's only a 10–7 game. Get out there and play hard."

After the kickoff, your offense continues to move the ball. Connor runs for seven yards. Then he gains five. You scramble for eight.

You lead the Gators to the Rams' 26-yard line. But a holding penalty stalls the drive, and you jog off the field without getting your team any points.

The fourth quarter begins with Sugar Valley moving toward the end zone. When they get to the 10-yard line, your defense finally tightens. The Rams can't punch it in for a touchdown, so they settle for a field goal. This extends their lead to six points.

When a team is losing in the fourth quarter, it adds a whole lot of pressure. The offense knows they must score. The defense knows they can't let the other team score. It makes everyone play tighter, and that's how mistakes happen.

If you can lead your team to a touchdown, you'll take that pressure off the Gators and put it on the Sugar Valley players.

Unfortunately, your drive manages only one first down. Briley has to punt the ball back to the Rams.

She boots it deep, but the returner might be the best in the state. He pinballs his way up the field, and at least six Gators miss their tackles on him.

Briley alone stands between him and the end zone— between him and almost certain defeat. The player cuts away from her, but she dives toward him. She grabs his feet and trips him. The good news is he doesn't score a touchdown. The bad news is he falls at the 16-yard line, within field goal range for the Rams.

"Come on, defense!" you shout. "No points!"

Your teammates rise to the occasion. They stuff the running back on three straight runs. But there's a reason Sugar Valley ran the ball three times—two reasons, actually. It takes more time off the clock, and they only need a field goal to put the game away.

The Rams line up for the kick. The center snaps the ball to the holder. He puts it down perfectly, and the kicker swings his leg.

You hear the *thump* of a perfectly kicked ball. You know that sound well from working with Briley.

But the first *thump* is almost immediately followed by a second, less perfect *thump*.

The Gator sideline erupts. Players cheer and begin to run around, laughing and clapping hands.

Santiago blocked the kick!

You look at the scoreboard. You're still only down by six. There's hope. But there's only 2:46 left to play. You know what needs to be done. You pray there's enough time to do it.

You try to surprise the Rams with a running play to Connor. It works the first time; he gains 13 yards. The second time, though, they stuff him behind the line of scrimmage.

Coach calls for a screen play. You dump a short pass to Kyle, and the rest of the team blocks for him. It's a great call, and it gains 26 yards.

You take a deep breath.

The Gators are at the Rams' 41-yard line. You hand off to Connor again. As he scoots ahead for nine yards, you sneak a peek at the clock: 51 seconds to go.

There isn't time to huddle up. You get your team to the line and use signals to call a play. You let your team know it's another handoff to Connor.

Nick hikes the ball, and Connor is tackled behind the line of scrimmage. The Sugar Valley fans begin to celebrate. They must think they have this won!

Just 32 seconds left. You don't have time to run the ball again. You need to throw it downfield. Of course, the defense knows this, too. They blitz an extra pass rusher, and you're forced to toss the football out of bounds.

The incomplete pass stops the clock, which allows you to catch your breath. But that also means it's fourth down. You only need one yard, which shouldn't be hard to get. But you don't have time for a one-yard play. You need to get 32 yards, into the end zone. And since it's fourth down, you have one play to do it.

This moment is going to take everything you have— everything you've worked so hard to become.

Add together all of your points.

If you have 15 or more points, go to page 151.

If you have 14 or fewer points, go to page 85.

You don't even want to know if the news is good or bad. This way, you can still hope the news is good—and that should get you through tonight's game.

"Don't tell me," you say. "I'll wait."

"No problem."

The team bus brings you to Valdosta. Brady and Nick lead some stretches. Then the team jogs around the field. You can't wait for the game to start. All of this down time has your mind racing. You keep thinking about what might be wrong with you. "Focus," you tell yourself. "Get your head in the game."

Tonight's opponent is the Valdosta Eagles. The team has skilled players and a rock-solid defense. The Gators need to play well to win.

Brady has been okayed by his doctor to play, so you're back to second string.

You only get in for three plays in the first quarter. In part, it's because the Eagles' defense is so tough. But also, the offense doesn't get a single first down. Brady limps in and out of the huddle. He misses a few wide-open throws—and the Eagles start crowding the line of scrimmage to stuff the run. It makes for a long quarter of wondering, *Why can't I write?*

Luckily, your team is playing better on defense. The Eagles put together a few good drives, but they never manage to score any points.

Half of the second quarter passes, and your defense starts to look tired. They allow Valdosta to march all the way down the field, not once but twice. The Eagles pull ahead by a score of 14–0.

Meanwhile, Brady continues to struggle. He nearly trips every time he hands off the ball, and his throws miss by as much as 10 yards. You can tell that his injury is bothering him—and his confidence is shaken.

"Jesse!" Coach Louis yells. "Can you do a better job out there?"

Can you? You don't know. You can't shake the feeling that something might be seriously wrong with you. You can't say that, though. You know what your coach wants to hear.

"Yes, Coach," you answer.

"Then go in for Brady and prove it," he says.

Four minutes remain in the first half. The Gators are on the 44-yard line. You call a running play in the huddle and then line up the team.

Connor gains two yards on first down. You get tackled for a loss of three yards on the next play. That makes it third down and 11 yards to go.

Coach signals for a pass play. When the football is snapped to you, you scurry back seven steps. You look toward Kyle, but he's covered by two Eagles. Your eyes shift focus to the other side of the field. Michael is wide open. Or is he? You're not sure. You don't trust yourself. If your brain won't let you write, maybe it won't let you make good choices on the field, either.

You hold the ball and keep scanning the field: left, middle, right . . .

The play takes too long. Two defensive linemen break through at the same instant. Both of them plow into you and drive you hard to the ground.

You hear the snap in your arm before you feel it. And then the pain comes. It's sharp, like someone is sticking you with a fork, over and over again.

You cry out in agony.

Coach Louis rushes to your side. Then a team doctor comes. Then the ambulance.

You don't need to be told. Your arm is broken. That means the end of your season. Win or lose, the Gators will have to continue without you.

Go to page 79.

You don't hesitate. You zip the football hard. It sails about seven yards over Kyle's head and lands safely out of bounds. It's a smart play. There's no reason to risk anything. The worst thing you could do right now is turn over the ball. The second worst thing would be to get sacked and lose yards.

Your team gets back into a huddle, and you call another passing play. "I'm only looking at Kyle, and I'm only throwing it if he's wide open," you tell your team. "A field goal still puts us in the lead."

If anyone can get open, it will be Kyle. He's quick, and he's tall. You take the ball from center, and you drop back, staring at your favorite target the whole way.

He runs the best route you've ever seen. He starts straight then darts toward the sideline, as if he's running an "out" pattern. For a moment, you think he's running the wrong route.

Suddenly, he stops, spins, and speeds toward the middle of the field. The cornerback doesn't stand a chance. In an instant, he goes from perfect coverage to three yards behind Kyle.

You spiral the football and hope with all of your might that Kyle finishes the play. He reaches out, catches the ball, and pulls it against his chest. Touchdown!

* * *

You don't remember everything about growing up with your dad, but you do remember the hunting trips. His favorite was hunting for quail. This fall's hunting season just opened, and you're not surprised when he invites you to join him.

He picks you up at 4 a.m. and drives for nearly an hour. By mid-morning, you each have one. Gary has some fantastic recipes for quail, so you're excited to get these home.

On the drive back, you both recap how you got your quails. (Part of the joy of hunting is telling the stories.) But then your dad gets quiet. He inhales a few times, like he's going to say something, but he blows out his breath and doesn't speak.

Finally, you ask, "What?"

"Well . . . I've been talking to Gary," he begins. He pauses. "Tina, too." Another pause. "Because of the wedding, you know, them getting married . . ."

What is he so nervous about?

"Well, I wanted to ask you . . . if it's okay for me to move in with you guys." He blows out his breath like he's been underwater for hours. "The plan would be for you and me to get our own place, some day. But we thought it would be easier if I moved into Gary's place first, for a while."

Silence follows. He's waiting for you to answer. But you don't know what to say. Still, you need to say something. What will you choose to do?

To tell him it's okay, go to page 121.

To tell him you're not ready, go to page 112.

You trust Michael. He's a good receiver, and he's made a lot of plays this year. You throw a dart that hits his gut. He cradles the catch against his body before turning to run.

He spins away from one defender, but another dives at his legs. Michael stumbles and falls, extending his arms as far as he can reach.

The referee marks him down at the 18 yard-line—one yard short of a first down. Coach calls for a field goal, and the game comes down to this play. If Briley makes it, the Gators win. If not, the season is over.

You take your position as holder, and Nick snaps the ball to you. You bobble it and then drop it. You try to grab it, but you can't get the football in the right place. Briley does her best to kick it anyway. You can tell by the dull thud of her foot connecting with the ball that it's not going to soar through the goal posts. The Gators' season is over.

Go to page 79.

You've played enough to know that holes in the line can close up quickly. You'll go with the original play. You hand off to Connor, and he dives into the end zone for a touchdown!

AWARD YOURSELF 1 SKILL POINT.

Briley kicks in her second extra point of the game, giving you a 14–13 lead.

The back and forth of the final quarter leans in the Falcons' favor. Coach yells at the defense to hold them. But it does little good. The Falcons eventually kick a field goal with just 43 seconds left. That puts the Gators behind, 14–16.

Of course, when there's still time on the clock, there's still hope. You trot onto the field, ready to move your team as quickly as you can.

You complete one pass. Then another. And another. You get all the way to the Falcons' 46-yard line. But there are just three seconds left on the clock—time for one last play. It's too far for a field goal. Your only chance is to heave a long pass into the end zone.

You don't get the opportunity. One of the defensive linemen pushes his way through and sacks you before you can throw the ball.

Game over. You really wanted this win. You wanted to show Coach Louis that you should be starting at QB.

Go to the next page.

On Saturday night, your uncle takes you out for dinner. While you eat, you talk about school, about Mrs. Beverage, and about football. You get the sense that he's nervous, though. What isn't he telling you?

After you finish eating, you finally find out.

He takes a deep breath. "I've got some news," he says, a smile stretching across his face. "I'm going to ask Tina to marry me."

Wow, that is news. What's even cooler is that he's telling you before he asks her. He truly must think of you as family. You clap your hands together. "Cool!"

His shoulders seem to relax, like he was afraid you wouldn't approve. "We've been dating for three years."

"When?" you say.

"When is the wedding?" he asks, looking unsure.

You laugh. "You have to ask her first. When are you going to do that?"

He looks down and starts fidgeting with his fingers. "Right. Well, I'm not sure."

If he's this nervous talking to you about it, how is he going to find the courage to ask her?

"I want to think of something romantic," he adds.

"Where did you two meet?"

He scratches his cheek. "Not very romantically. She was a customer. I fixed her dining room lights."

You sit for a minute, thinking. "Is your boss a nice guy?" you ask.

"Oh, yes, he's real nice."

"Would he let you borrow a bucket truck?"

"Of course," Uncle Gary answers.

You grin. "You could lift her up near some treetops or something and propose up there."

Uncle Gary laughs heartily. "What a great idea! How did you think of that?"

You smile proudly. "I read a lot at the library."

Uncle Gary could be a lamp, the way he lights up. But his smile soon fades. "I've also been thinking about the wedding . . . and who to invite. One of the guests would be . . . your dad."

That word takes a minute for you to swallow.

Uncle Gary waits for it to sink in before he goes on. "I decided to track him down. It took me a couple of months, but I found him about an hour from here."

You look down at your lap. Your mind is a whirring blur of thoughts and emotions. It makes you a little bit dizzy.

"Do you want to see him?" your uncle asks.

You glance back up at him. You start to answer, but you're not sure what to say. Dad left you and Mom. He wasn't there for her battle—or for her funeral. He wasn't there for the *after*. He wasn't there for you! The thought of seeing him makes you angry. You wonder if it could lead to trouble.

On the other hand, he is your dad. Your mom is gone, and he's all that's left of what you thought was a happy family. Maybe seeing him will also bring a part of her back to you.

What will you choose to do?

To see your dad, go to page 110.

To tell Uncle Gary, "No," go to page 86.

"I'll see him in here, I guess," you say.

Uncle Gary offers a smile. "I'll get him."

You stand and go to the window. You shove your hands in your pockets and look outside. A few kids are playing across the street, and another neighbor is working in his yard. You wish you were out there, too.

"Hey, Jesse." Your dad sounds just like his brother.

You don't turn from the window. "Hey."

"I hear your football team made it to the semifinals. Congratulations"

You nod. "Thanks."

You hear his steps, and then the bed creaks.

"I took that picture of you and Mom. We went for a picnic at the park. You loved being outside."

You turn from the window and stare at your dad. He's lost a lot of weight, and he looks . . . exhausted.

"Do you know I lived outside for a year?" you ask, making it sound like an accusation.

He looks down and nods.

"Because you left," you say, "and Mom died?"

He doesn't look up. "I never knew she was sick. Gary's the one who told me . . . after she passed away." He wipes his cheeks. "I'm so—" He chokes, tries again. "I'm so sorry, Jesse."

"I'm hungry," you say and walk out of your room.

You find Gary and Tina in the kitchen, leaning against the counter, talking.

"Can we eat?" you ask.

"Of course," Tina says.

Your dad follows you in, and Tina hands him a plate. Everyone gets their food and sits at the table.

You don't say anything, just eat and listen to your uncle and your dad talk about their jobs. The topic shifts to Gary and Tina's wedding, and there's even a bit of laughter—from everyone except you.

AWARD YOURSELF 1 CONFIDENCE POINT.

Go to page 94.

Kyle has been a great receiver all season. Now, when you need a play the most, he's the one to go to. You aim the ball at his numbers and throw.

The cornerback tips the pass, but the football floats up, not down. This allows Kyle to reach up and grab it. The cornerback tries to do the same, but he's not quick enough. The effort causes him to fall, leaving Kyle all alone. He practically jogs to the end zone. No one is close enough to catch him.

The quirky play gives the Gators the lead . . . and the win!

The next week of practice goes well, and Coach says, "I'm confident we can win the quarterfinal game."

School goes much better, thanks to Mrs. Beverage. Briley, too. She helps you with homework almost every day after practice.

At home, Uncle Gary's smile never fades. He and Tina busily plan their December wedding. No one ever mentions your dad.

Your quarterfinal contest is in the town of Sixes; it has the nicest, newest field. Your opponent is a familiar one: the Canton Coyotes. Conversation often shifts to when Briley got tackled by one of their players.

Your heart feels ready to leap out of your chest when Coach Louis calls your name to start. After your last performance, you expected it—but it's still nice to hear.

The Coyotes receive the kickoff to start the game. It is apparent from the very first drive that they are a much tougher opponent than Fairmont was. Their possession takes them to the end zone, giving them a 7–0 lead.

Your offense puts together a nice drive of your own. You don't quite get to the goal line, though. Briley kicks a 26-yard field goal.

The Coyotes move the football again. They hold the ball for nine plays and eventually add a field goal. At the end of the first quarter, it's 3–10.

The second quarter does not begin well for you. You fumble on a handoff to Connor and are lucky to recover it. Then, on the next play, you throw an interception.

The Coyotes' offense steps in while you stomp to the sideline. You expect to get yelled at by Coach Louis, but he doesn't say a thing.

The Coyotes turn your mistake into a touchdown. That makes it a lopsided 3–17 game. If your team doesn't turn things around fast, this will end in a blowout.

Fortunately, someone on your team finally makes a play. Kyle returns the kickoff 78 yards, all the way down to the 10-yard line.

The offense doesn't muster even one more yard. Briley boots another field goal.

The score remains 6–17 until halftime.

"Gentlemen and Lady," Coach Louis begins, "this game is not over. You've beaten this team once. You can do it again." As he goes on, he stays mostly positive. But he loses his patience, at times, too. His frustration is as apparent as the sweat under his armpits.

Before he exits, he glances at you, and then he looks at your backup. "Brady, you're in at quarterback."

Ouch. If you didn't know better, you'd think that someone punched you in the gut. Your cheeks grow warm, and you bite your bottom lip. You don't want to say anything you might regret.

Go to the next page.

On his first drive, Brady leads the offense up the field. He makes it look so easy; you check to see if he's playing Canton's backups!

The drive stalls at the 11-yard line, and Coach opts for Briley to kick a field goal again.

You run onto the field and take your place as holder. Nick snaps the ball, and you place it perfectly. Briley kicks it up, up, and through the goal posts.

This time the dirty Coyote player—the one who went after Briley—kicks you hard in the side. Then he laughs at you.

Anger rises in you like boiling water in a pot. This guy is a bully, and you can't let him get away with it. You're frustrated. You're embarrassed. You're ready for a fight.

How many teamwork points do you have?

If you have 5 or more, go to page 105.

If you have 4 or fewer, go to page 73.

"Brady, you're a good quarterback. This isn't about talent or skill. The problem is you're hurt. So you're not giving us the best chance to win. Tonight, I'm the better option for our team."

Brady doesn't answer. He just turns and leaves the locker room. You follow him to the field.

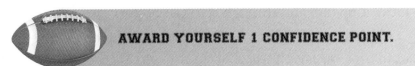

AWARD YOURSELF 1 CONFIDENCE POINT.

The Eagles score again to start the third quarter: The kicker hits a field goal from the 15-yard line, making it a 0–17 game.

Now, it's your turn.

You connect on a pass to your tight end for 16 yards. Then you run the very same play again, and it goes for 11. Two plays after that, Connor takes the handoff, squirts through the line, and dashes 50 yards for a touchdown! Briley's extra point makes the score 7–17.

The Gators' first score of the night seems to wake up the defense. Truc forces a fumble and recovers the ball on the Eagles' 24-yard line.

You lead the offense back onto the field.

Coach Louis calls a pass play to Kyle, but he can't get open. You look toward Michael; he's covered, too. There's nowhere to throw the ball, and your linemen can't block forever. You know what to do: run.

You dodge a tackle, break free from a linebacker who grabs your jersey, and dive across the goal line.

Touchdown!

You jump off the ground and run to every teammate on the field, slapping high-fives and yelling excitedly. You glance at your uncle, and he's standing, clapping, and cheering.

You force yourself to settle down. The game's not over, and the Gators are still down by three.

Rosso's defense again gets the job done. Valdosta doesn't make it past the 40-yard line. They punt the ball to your team, and you move deep into the Eagles' end of the field.

When it's first down on the 18-yard line, Coach calls for a pass to Michael in the end zone. You fake a run to Connor. Then you pump the ball toward Kyle, like you're going to throw it. The defense falls for it, and Michael stands wide open. You throw one of your best passes of the night . . . touchdown!

The clock runs out on the Eagles before they reach midfield. The Rosso Gators win!

7
MRS. BEVERAGE

On Monday, you still feel unbeatable thanks to the big win. It makes being at school seem a little better.

Before your first class, you meet your new teacher, Mrs. Beverage. You can't help but ask, "Is that really your last name?"

"I asked my husband the very same thing when I met him." She laughs. The curls in her hair bob.

You laugh with her.

"All right," she says. "You'll be in a class with me and a dozen other students for 30 minutes a day. We'll work on writing. Do you have any questions about that?"

You shake your head. "Not now."

She smiles. "Good, see you back here at 11:40."

The morning is filled with frustration. Your classes continue to pile on the writing assignments, and you forget your good mood. By the time you get to Mrs. Beverage's class, you don't feel very smart.

Instead of writing with pen and paper, you work on keyboarding skills. The half hour zips by. If only the rest of your classes could be so enjoyable.

Friday brings another game, this time against the Kennesaw Falcons.

"Lady and gentlemen," Coach Louis says, "do not go into this game overconfident. Kennesaw is a good team. Play hard from the first whistle and don't let up."

You're tonight's quarterback. But Brady is okay to play. He puts on his uniform and looks healthy.

The first quarter goes about as poorly as a quarter ever has for you. You fumble the ball once and only complete two passes—both interceptions to the Falcons.

"Jesse," says Coach, "take a seat. We're going to give Brady a try."

Now you know how Brady feels when you take over for him: somewhere between embarrassed and mad.

The offense doesn't improve with Brady out there. It's like there's a wall at midfield, and your team can't break through it.

At halftime, you trail, 0–13.

Early in the third quarter, your luck starts to turn. The Gator defense scoops up a fumble at their 40-yard line and runs it in for a touchdown.

When you get the ball again, Coach sends you onto the field, instead of Brady. This time, you pick away at the defense. You complete eight short passes in a row, driving all the way to the Falcons' two-yard line.

There, three straight running plays gain zero yards, making it fourth down and goal to go.

Coach calls for another handoff to Connor, but the plays that got you this far have been passes. Still, you don't want to make Coach mad. You keep the play.

Nick snaps the football, and you notice a defensive tackle slip and fall. It creates an instant hole in the line, easy for you to run through. Should you forget the play and run it yourself? Or will you stick with the plan and hand the ball to Connor? What will you choose to do?

To run the ball, go to page 114.

To give the ball to Connor, go to page 135.

Coach signals for a deep pass. In your heart, you know it's still possible to win this game.

When Nick snaps the ball, you scan the field. Kyle, Michael, and three other receivers dash to the end zone. Eight Rams are waiting to cover them. Three rushers try to sack you. They're blocked by your linemen.

You've played football your whole life. You've always practiced as hard as you've played. Your instincts for the game are good. You know that the defensive backs are ready. But your odds of success grow, the longer you wait to pass.

You scramble to your left . . . and wait. You jog to your right . . . and wait. Your offensive line can easily handle three rushers—but not forever. The defensive end to your right finally breaks through. You're out of time.

You roll away from him, looking for an open window in the end zone. You spot one. There are a lot of defenders behind the goal line, but all that time has caused them to bunch up. A receiver notices it, too. He runs toward that window in the defense, and you throw the football as hard and as fast as you can.

The ball zips down the field in a tight, straight line. It arrives in that window at the same instant your wide receiver does. The throw is a little too hard, a little too high. Your teammate jumps and extends his arms. He snags the ball out of the air and pulls it into his body, just as two defensive backs slam against him.

He falls to the ground, but he doesn't let go.

The referee looks down at Brady Sanchez, and he nods. "Touchdown!"

You leap into the air! You run over to your nearest lineman and jump on his back! You're so excited, you don't know what to do!

You look at the scoreboard, and you remember that it's only a tie game. There's still an extra point to kick.

Briley trots onto the field. Her expression is casual, like this is just another kick. At that moment, you feel certain that she will make it.

Nick snaps the ball. You place it. Briley kicks . . .

EPILOGUE

At the last practice, you admit to your teammates the truth about your homelessness. No one gets mad. In fact, they give you a standing ovation for coming back.

You and Dad share a lot of time with Uncle Gary and Tina, but they're busy planning a wedding. It's time for you and Dad to find an apartment to rent.

Briley hangs with you every day. And your classes with Mrs. Beverage have been a game-changer, too. You actually enjoy coming to school now. It turns out that dysgraphia isn't the end of the world.

As a state champion, you've become a local hero. You plan to use your new fame—to help get Rosso's homeless teenagers off the streets and into school.

YOU WIN

CONGRATULATIONS!

CHOOSE TO WIN!

Read the fast-paced, action-packed stories. Make the right choices. Find your way to the "winning" ending!

Back to Pass
Goal-Minded
Out at Home
Save the Season!

YOU'RE THE MAIN CHARACTER. YOU MAKE THE CHOICES.
CAN YOU SURVIVE?

20,000 Leagues Under the Sea
Adventures of Perseus
Adventures of Sherlock Holmes
Call of the Wild
Dracula
King Solomon's Mines
Merry Adventures of Robin Hood
Three Musketeers
Treasure Island
Twelve Labors of Hercules

about the author

Lisa M. Bolt Simons has been a teacher for more than 20 years, and she's been a writer for as long as she can remember. She has written four "Choose to Win!" middle grade novels, more than 25 nonfiction children's books, and a history book, *Faribault Woolen Mill: Loomed in the Land of Lakes*. She is currently working on several other projects. Both her nonfiction and fiction works have been recognized with various accolades.

In her spare time, Lisa loves to read and to scrapbook. Originally from Colorado, Lisa currently lives in Minnesota with her husband, Dave, and she's the mom of twins, Jeri and Anthony. She was a busy sports mom for over a decade.

CONFIDENCE:

SKILL:

SPEED:

TEAMWORK:

TALENT POINTS:

CONFIDENCE:

SKILL:

SPEED:

TEAMWORK:

TALENT POINTS:

CONFIDENCE:

SKILL:

SPEED:

TEAMWORK:

TALENT POINTS: